LAST KNOWN POSITION

STEVEN GALE

DEDICATION

To Hannah and Aaron, you two are my heroes
To my wonderful wife Sally
To Liam, Sienna, and Wolf never stop dreaming
To my best friend growing up, my little brother Jon

First paperback edition April 2021
First ebook edition April 2021
Print ISBN: 978-1-7367487-0-1
Ebook ISBN: 978-1-7367487-1-8

Book cover and interior design by JohnEdgar.Design
Published by Agragape Publications

THERE IS SOMETHING
IN THOSE MOUNTAINS
MANGLER2

STEVEN GALE

STORYTELLER & AUTHOR

As a kid Steven would hide behind his dad's chair during the TV show 'The Night Stalker'. Having grown up during arguably the best era in motion picture history, he believes that helped him develop the art of storytelling. He feels today's special effects have robbed people of developing their own imagination.

Steven is the father of two active duty soldiers and husband to a wonderful wife. He loves hiking in the mountains and doing research for upcoming Mangler books

LAST KNOWN POSITION

STEVEN GALE

CONTENTS

Chapter One:
A NEW DAY

1545 HOURS
PRESENT-DAY
FORT CAMPBELL, KENTUCKY

"Are we ever going to take off?" Doyle asks Leon as they sit in the Learjet on the runway.

"I'm not sure what the holdup is, Doyle," Leon tells him looking at his watch. They feel the plane start moving but it is turning back towards the hangar. "Something's going on buddy," Leon says looking out the window. "They're opening the doors to the hangar, I guess this operation is over before we even got started."

Doyle looks over past Leon and out the window, "Looks that way."

The jet pulls into the hangar as they close the doors behind it. One of the operators sitting near the front of the plane opens the door and drops the steps down. Doyle feels his phone vibrate, he pulls his phone out and reads the text:

The boy has been found. Stand down.

"Operation canceled," he tells Leon.

"Get used to this Doyle, it happens a lot," Leon says walking towards the front of the plane.

"What? Me finding them so quick?" Doyle asks as he follows him.

"That's right. Boy! You're good Doyle," Leon says laughing with his high-pitched laugh.

Doyle looks at him shaking his head, "You should have known that by now." The two guys climb off the plane and grab their travel bags.

"Sir, I'll pull your truck inside and we'll load your gear into it for you," one of the operators says to Doyle.

"Okay. Thanks. Leon I'm going to go talk to Stevens," Doyle tells him as he starts walking towards the office door.

Leon looks over at him, "Wait just a second, Doyle."

Doyle ignores him and opens the office door. Once inside he notices that the office is completely empty. Doyle stops and looks around, *what the hell?* He walks into the adjoining office, where the doughnuts and coffee were...empty as well.

Leon jogs through the door, finally catching up with him.

"What's going on?" Doyle asks him.

"You didn't give me time to explain things to you," responds Leon out of breath. Doyle walks over closer, "We haven't been gone for no more than thirty minutes. Where's Stevens?"

"Stevens doesn't exist," Leon replies.

"Excuse me?" asks Doyle.

Leon raises his hands up, "Just let me explain."

Doyle crosses his arms, "I'm listening."

"That guy or the guy this time works for the head of our Patriots group. Stevens is the code name they use but it's almost never the same man," explains Leon. "You'll never see or meet the people in charge, they use doubles or mid-level guys to do the footwork. Most of the people at the top never leave their home or office. Come on, let's go to your truck so we can talk in private," he tells Doyle as he turns around and walks out of the empty office.

Doyle follows him out of the office and into the hangar where his truck is parked. Leon climbs in on the passenger's side, just after Doyle gets in and closes the driver's side door a man in the back seat sits up and throws a rope around Doyle's neck. He pulls it tight as Doyle grabs onto it pulling with all his might. He swings his left fist over his head trying to hit his assailant. They struggle for a few seconds as Doyle starts to turn blue. "Enough!" yells Leon.

Doyle falls forward, his head resting against the steering wheel. Doyle slowly sits up rubbing his neck, he looks into the rear-view mirror. "What?" he says. Looking back at him in the mirror is Aaron, Bullseye's brother.

"Doyle. I know you let your guard down getting into the truck because I am with you. But you must always check the backseat. Don't trust anyone now," Leon explains to him. "There are people that will

be looking to kill you if they find out you work with us or even just talk to us."

Doyle turns to look at Aaron, "How's this possible? You've been dead for almost thirty years."

Aaron reaches up and pats him on the shoulder, "I didn't hurt your neck, did I?" Doyle rubs his throat, then responds, "I'll be fine."

"I'm your go-to guy, your advisor...your boss," Aaron explains. "I'm the one that chose you over a list of exceptionally fine candidates. The only reason we didn't bring you in earlier is because of the terminal illness Susan contracted from working at ground zero."

"But I saw your dead body when they brought you back to the base," Doyle tells him.

"It was a fake body, Doyle," Aaron replies. "Although, I was severely injured. I spent six weeks in the hospital recovering."

Doyle looks Aaron in the eyes, "Is Bullseye still alive too?" he asks.

"Unfortunately, he is not," Aaron says softly. "They killed him because of me. They found out I was working with the patriots. They used you to get to him, Miller used you."

"Why not just come after you? Why Bullseye? He was a good kid...a fine soldier," responds Doyle.

Aaron looks out the window of the truck, "That's how they work. They want you to suffer as much as possible before they set you up to go to prison or they kill you. I do want to thank you for taking care of my baby brother. He looked up to you."

"You don't owe me a thank-you. I enjoyed every minute of working with him," replies Doyle. "I just can't help but think I could have saved him that night," Doyle says looking down at the floorboard.

"The past can't be undone, Doyle. We must keep moving forward. Now, you will only deal with me and Leon, no one above us. In fact, we are denying that you even work with us. That way your family will be safe," Aaron explains to him.

"We're all back on the same team," Leon chimes in. "The only difference is the entire world thinks Aaron and I are dead," Leon says laughing.

"I guess I have that going for me," replies Doyle as he turns and looks at Aaron, "So, Miller put the hit on Bullseye, Correct?"

"That's correct," answers Aaron.

"Well. I guess I'm going to have to kill Miller then," Doyle says slowly nodding his head.

"If the opportunity presents itself you are clear to do that. But that is not your objective," Aaron says handing him a small notebook.

"What's this?" Doyle asks, grabbing the notebook.

"That's the information on the person you're protecting right now," Aaron tells him.

Doyle looks back at him and asks, "Protecting?"

Leon turns and faces Doyle, "That's correct. They're on the SGs list to be removed."

Doyle looks at Leon and then at Aaron and asks, "Removed? Meaning killed?" Aaron nods, "That's correct. But not if you're protecting them."

Aaron opens the truck door, "Just like I was protecting you during the search for the Wolfgang boy. Except you will not be wearing a suit like I was. You almost saw me that stormy night...luckily you thought your dog was barking at those deer." Aaron steps out of the truck, "Leon will fill you in on the details. I'll see you in a few months, be safe." Aaron walks off and exits through a back door.

"What...what did he just say?" Doyle asks Leon. "He was on the ground during that search?"

Leon smiles at Doyle, "Getting weird uh? Now let's get going, I'm riding with you to Chattanooga."

Shaking his head Doyle replies, "Weird isn't the word for it, son." He starts the truck and puts it in drive, "You've got a lot of explaining to do on our way home." After Doyle says that Leon lets out a high-pitched laugh.

As they drive through the base Doyle looks over at Leon, "I'll tell you, I sure do miss the life."

Leon nods in agreement, "I hear you, brother...I hear ya."

They pull up to the gate and the Staff Sergeant on duty walks to the truck. "How are you, Sergeant?" Doyle asks.

"I'm good sir. How are you, sir?" he replies.

Doyle reaches out of the truck window and shakes his hand,

"Thank you for your service." He notices that the sergeant has an Operation Iraqi Freedom ribbon on, "What unit in Iraq?"

"Sir, the 18th Military Police Brigade," the sergeant tells him.

"Of course. Me and my buddy here, we were with the 75th in both wars in Iraq and Afghanistan," Doyle tells him pointing at Leon.

The sergeant leans down and looks over at Leon then back to Doyle, "Thank you both for your service too."

Doyle hands him the paperwork that Stevens left in the truck for the gate. After the sergeant looks them over, he hands them back, "You guys have a great day." He says as he turns and walks back into the guard shack and raises the gate.

Doyle turns left onto Alt-41 and follows it to interstate 24 south to Nashville. Leon waits for Doyle to set the cruise control, "I guess the first thing you need to know, is that Allen did survive. He's alive and well in protective custody."

Doyle looks at him in shock, "What? No kidding?"

Leon reaches over and slaps Doyle's leg, "Damn straight! You kicked butt. The best thing you did was ignoring Joe's order that no one was to camp out that last night."

Doyle looks at him, "That was just a gut feeling. Besides, when I'm out on a search I call my own shots."

"Joe was compromised. He was getting pressure from DC. They didn't want anyone out there that night so they could finish the job," explains Leon.

"I thought he seemed rattled. How did they get Allen out of the hospital in Asheville?" Doyle asks.

"They never took him to that hospital. They did the switch-arue, two different helicopters went to Asheville while the one carrying Allen turned west and landed at Camp McClellan in Alabama," Leon explains.

"That's amazing…Hell yeah!" shouts Doyle slamming his fist on the steering wheel.

Leon laughs, "It's amazing what we can do when the government is not calling the shots. Mankind can do extraordinary things when they're not in bondage," he looks out the window before continuing. "From what I heard; Miller was pissed when that helicopter landed without the boy."

Doyle watching the truck in front of them says, "That changes everything."

Leon smiles, "Amen brother."

"So, who is this person I'm going to be protecting?" asks Doyle.

Leon reaches into the back seat and grabs a small box that was sitting on the floorboard.

"What's that?" Doyle asks.

"Hand me your phone," Leon tells him. After Doyle hands him his phone, Leon puts both his and Doyle's into the box.

"This box is specially lined to keep anyone from being able to access

our phones and listening to us," explains Leon.

Doyle looks over at him, "So, why didn't you put our phones in there before you told me about Allen?"

Leon laughs again, "They already know that. Okay. The subject is a forty-eight-year-old woman from California. Her name is Amy Leek, she is the now ex-wife of California congressman Chuck Leek."

"Why am I protecting a congressman's ex-wife?" Doyle asks, sounding confused.

"We'll. You see, this Mr. Leek is a real bad guy. He's part of the SG, a real mean bastard too," Leon tells him as he pulls his small notebook out of his pocket. Leon opens it to a section with notes about Amy, "She's a fire ecologist."

Doyle looks at him, "So, she studies wild-fires. Big deal."

"Hang on, let me finish. She evidently threatened to spill the beans on Chuck's dealings with the SG," Leon adds. "We intercepted plans of a hit on her by the SG," he tells Doyle.

"Really?" Doyle asks then says, "It's sounding more interesting now."

"Yeah. She is part of a scientific study taking place in a few months at Yosemite National Park," Leon adds.

"Yosemite, that's a tough place for missing people. I consulted on a search there some years back, they still to this day haven't found anything from that person," Doyle tells him.

"As you know, that's exactly what the SG uses to hide behind...natural phenomenon's," Leon says.

"Will she know that we are there or are we ghosts?" asks Doyle.

"We're ghosts brother," Leon tells him.

"Perfect. Just how I like it," replies Doyle.

Leon puts his notebook back in his pocket, "The hard part is getting you on the ground without anyone seeing you. We are going to fly you out there, but we will not fly this truck there. We have a person coming in to drive this truck around the Smoky Mountains that looks a lot like you," explains Leon.

"Good-looking guy eh?" Doyle asks laughing.

Leon lets out his high-pitched laugh, "Yeah, he's a pretty boy alright."

Doyle gives him a funny look, "Laugh it up."

After Leon stops laughing, he says, "You'll need to grow your deployment beard back."

Doyle nods in agreement. The two guys stop talking as Doyle maneuvers through the Nashville traffic. Once they get back to the open highway Doyle asks, "When Bullseye was shot down, who were the Taliban that were seen running from the site?"

Leon pauses, "They were SG operators used to deceive the support Apaches into thinking the shot came from the ground."

"That's why Miller wouldn't give them the permission to fire..."

Doyle says nodding his head. "And I'm guessing that's also why he wouldn't let us use the different Chinook?"

"That's correct. Aaron will give you more details about that night at a later date," Leon tells him.

The song 'American Girl' comes on the radio, Doyle turns the volume up. "Love this song," he tells Leon.

Leon, who has a great singing voice starts singing along, "Oh yeah... All right. Take it easy baby..."

Doyle smiles then thinks, *Just like old times.*

1922 HOURS
PRESENT-DAY
CHATTANOOGA, TENNESSEE

"Oh, my goodness. That food smells so good!" Leon exclaims walking towards the entrance to the restaurant.

"I'm starving too," Doyle replies.

"Age before beauty," Leon tells him as he opens the door and motions for Doyle to go ahead.

Doyle walks up to the hostess, "Table for two ma'am."

"Right this way gentlemen," she says grabbing two menus.

After the hostess seats them Doyle gets up, "I'm going to go wash up, be back in just a bit." Leon gives him a thumbs-up as he starts to look over the menu.

He watches Doyle walk into the bathroom then pulls his phone out. "It's all going very well. We're at the steakhouse by the Hamilton Place Mall, pick me up in forty-five minutes."

"You know what you want?" Doyle asks him as he returns from the bathroom.

"Oh yeah, I'm a breakfast any time of the day kind of guy," Leon replies.

They place their orders then Doyle asks, "How much do you know about those suits?"

Leon takes a drink of his tea, "Not a whole lot. But I do know they use your DNA somehow. The suit has to be set up for the operator or something like that."

"So, you've never been in one?" asks Doyle.

"No. That's way above my pay grade. The only time I've ever seen one was when they saved me."

Doyle looks surprised, "Really? I figured you'd been around them more."

Leon shakes his head, "No. Their use is top secret. Even if it is used on a job, you are on, I doubt you'll even know it."

The waitress delivers their food to the table, "Anything else gentlemen?" She asks after she sits the plates down.

"No ma'am. Everything looks great," Leon says.

After she walks off Doyle asks, "How high up the chain is Aaron?"

Leon grabs his napkin, wipes his mouth, then replies, “Way up it. He moved up considerably after 9/11 when they fired a lot of Patriots.”

“What? For not stopping the attacks?” Doyle asks.

“That’s correct. That was the SGs shining moment. However, many within our group thought it should have been stopped,” Leon tells him.

“When you say fired, what does that mean?” asks Doyle.

Leon puts his elbows on the table and his hands together. Wringing his hands and looking directly into Doyle’s eyes, he responds, “Executed.”

Doyle sits back in his chair, “Damn.” He looks around the restaurant then back at Leon, “They don’t mess around uh?”

The two sit there for a moment staring at each other before Leon breaks the silence, “The way it should be, don’t you agree?”

Doyle puts a pill in his mouth, takes a drink of lemonade then answers, “Yeah.”

Leon takes a drink then looks at Doyle, “So much from that day is still classified, even for our group. Almost everyone believes it was an inside job but cannot figure out how they pulled it off. Oh, by the way. How’s your PTSD?” he asks.

Doyle replies, “That was a huge operation to run with everyone watching. It’s okay, as long as I continue to take my medication.”

Leon looks around the restaurant, “I’d keep the fact you have to take medicine to control it to yourself. Although, I’m sure they know by now.”

Doyle smiles, “I’ll keep that in mind.”

The two guys finish their supper without any more conversation.

“Check please,” Leon tells the waitress. “This is where I leave you, Doyle.”

Doyle looks at him, “What do you mean?”

“I have a ride that just pulled in. We have business to do in Atlanta. You go home and rest, spend time with Susan, and grow that beard. I’ll contact you with the details of the trip in a few weeks.”

“Okay. I can do that,” replies Doyle.

Leon leans forward, “Now listen, I know you’ll tell Susan some things, but don’t give her too many details about where you’re going. For her own safety, okay?”

Doyle drops a ten-dollar bill on the table, “No worries buddy.”

Leon stands up, “You hang tight for a few minutes. Have another glass of lemonade, just give us time to get down the road a-ways.”

“No problem,” Doyle says as he shakes Leon’s hand.

“Assume they are always watching,” Leon replies, then walks away.

“Ma’am, could I have another drink please?” Doyle asks the waitress. “And the dessert menu too, please.”

After he eats a slice of cheesecake, he lays another ten-dollar bill on

the table. "Thank you, ma'am," he says getting up and walking out of the restaurant. Once outside he stops and looks the new truck over good.

I do not like this new truck; he thinks as he grabs the bug shield and inspects to see how to remove it.

This will fit on my old truck.

He stands there nodding for a bit before climbing in and driving off.

2100 HOURS
PRESENT-DAY
DOYLE & SUSAN'S HOME

As Doyle pulls in the driveway, he can hear Gunner barking from inside the house.

"Wow. Look at that fancy truck," Susan says walking out onto the front porch.

Gunner runs out the door and down the steps with Susan. Doyle climbs out of the truck and rubs Gunner, "Hey, Buddy." He says walking over to Susan and giving her a hug.

"I wasn't expecting you back for a week or so," she says.

"The operation was canceled. They found the boy," he tells her as they climb up the front steps. "Looks like I don't have an operation for a few months," he says as they sit down in the rocking chairs on the porch.

"What are you going to do until then?" she asks.

"I have a few SAR classes that I'm doing. Other than that, I don't know, maybe some fishing," he replies. "Oh. I have to grow my beard back too. I think I'll also grow my horseshoe around my head since nothing will grow on the top of my head," he tells her laughing.

She looks at him puzzled, "Why?"

Doyle kicks his boots off, "They don't want me looking like me. Plus, the hair around my head will connect to my beard and make me look a lot older with all the grays."

"That shouldn't take you very long. You can almost grow a beard overnight," she says.

"True," he replies. Gunner lays down between the two rocking chairs and closes his eyes. They sit there rocking and looking at the half-moon hanging over the lake.

"I guess it really is a new day, uh?" she asks him.

"Yes, it is," he replies, pulling his hat over his eyes and putting his feet up on the handrail.

A cool breeze blows through the valley.

The moon seems to move in and out from behind the clouds in its path.

A Whip-poor-will can be heard off in the distance.

The peaceful sounds are interrupted by Doyle's snoring.

Susan continues to rock as something stirs in the forest.

Chapter Two:
CHANGE IN PLANS

1909 HOURS
TWO-WEEKS LATER, PRESENT-DAY
MARYVILLE, TENNESSEE, SHERIFF'S OFFICE

"Okay, gentlemen. This is the first class in the training program I will be bringing to you on the first Tuesday of every month through July. Tonight's hour for February we're going to be talking about hunters," Doyle explains to the classroom of cops.

"It is important to determine what type of game the hunter is after. In other words, are they hunting in a blind or in a tree?"

"Seventy percent of the calls you'll respond to regarding hunters are of them being lost. Although most hunters hate when a searcher uses the word 'lost' when they are found. They're a proud bunch," Doyle says as the room erupts in laughter.

"Hunters being too focused on following the game or wounded game is the leading cause of getting lost. Nightfall comes in a close second."

"Some hunters will avoid rescuers out of fear of fines or even being embarrassed. Thirty-three percent will self-rescue and find their way out of the mountains on their own," says Doyle as he turns on the projector.

"Most hunters will travel with few provisions but plenty of ammo. Ninety percent of them know to give three whistle blasts or fire three shots if they are lost. Our response in search and rescue is two whistles or fire two shots."

"I wish I could tell you that it's rare to have to search for a hunter that doesn't know to fire three shots...but I can't. Sometimes a hunter has been separated from his weapon, he has fallen down a slope or something along those lines, but it is exceedingly rare. They tend to travel at night or prior to first light," he tells them as he points his laser pointer at the chart.

"Look at the chart for survivability. Uninjured in the wilderness have an eighty-six percent chance of survival, while only nine percent if injured..."

As Doyle is wrapping up the hour, he sits a stack of binders on the front table, "Guys if you would on your way out grab a binder. It has six of the most interesting cases of lost hunters I have been a part of in my career. Four of the hunters were found days later, one's body was found three months later. The last case still keeps me up some nights, we never found him or any of his belongings or any trace of him."

Doyle walks to the back of the conference room to shake hands

with the cops as they exit.

"Thank you, guys. My number is on my business card inside the binder, call if you have any questions."

As he packs up his materials Aaron walks into the conference room, "Good job as usual Doyle."

Doyle looks up and asks, "What brings you here?"

"We have a new development. Need you out in the field as soon as possible," Aaron explains.

Aaron walks to the front of the room and takes a seat, "I was listening out in the hallway. You're exceptionally good."

Doyle closes his briefcase, "Thanks. But it's difficult standing up here talking about the reasons hunters go missing and I can't include that a handful of government nuts are running around in the forest killing people." He looks at Aaron, "Conspiracy theory, right?"

Aaron laughs, "Right. You know the CIA invented that phrase in 1963 to help cover up the fact that they just assassinated the President of the United States."

"Seems like I read that somewhere," Doyle replies before asking, "So, what are the new developments?"

Aaron stands up and walks over to Doyle, "It's Amy Leek's brother. He disappeared yesterday in the Sierra National Forest south of Yosemite."

Doyle looks at him, "So. Why is he important?"

"Well, let us just say he's eccentric. He claims to be a prophet from God, he goes by the name of Jonah now. His real name is Corey Prine, he once ran a small church in Wasco, California," explains Aaron.

"Oh boy! That is all I need," exclaims Doyle.

Aaron continues, "He has worked for the government for decades programming much of their top-secret software. They believe he hacked into one of the SG's computers and downloaded some files. We had originally thought Amy was the SG's target, but we now feel that was misinformation. I do not believe they have gotten to him yet, I guess he went up in the mountains to hide or God knows what," Aaron tells him.

"Her study in Yosemite is still a month off, right?" Doyle asks.

"It is. But she is trying to move it up to next week," answers Aaron.

"Interesting. So, you want me to find the preacher and do what?" asks Doyle as he starts walking towards the door.

"Find him, then bring him to Edwards Air Force Base," Aaron says following him out of the room.

"Why Edwards?" Doyle asks looking directly at Aaron.

"That is where he has worked most of his career there at the sister base," replies Aaron.

"Sister base? I didn't know there was a sister base tied to Edwards." Doyle says tilting his head to the left.

"that's all I can say at this time Doyle. Just get to him before a SG operator in a suit does."

"Right, that should be easy enough, me and a preacher in a fight against an invisible suit. Hell, that sounds winnable," Doyle says.

As they walk outside Aaron replies, "This preacher might surprise you. You are the right man for the job, he will trust you and listen to you. He's an ex-Navy Frogman."

Doyle stops dead in his tracks, "Really?"

Aaron smiles, "Yes, really. I thought that might change your outlook."

Doyle opens the back door of his truck and places his briefcase on the back seat then asks, "Do you know if he's alone?"

"As far as we know he is. Although we have not been able to confirm that," answers Aaron.

"I'm assuming that the SG has already started searching for him?" asks Doyle.

"We have to assume they have, or at least they will be before we can get you there," Aaron tells him handing him an envelope.

"What's this?" Doyle asks.

"Your plane ticket to Vegas, credit cards, and cash for this operation," Aaron explains.

"Vegas?" Doyle asks, sounding confused.

Aaron nods his head, "Yes. We are flying you there for a search

and rescue seminar, or at least that is the cover story. Instead, we will transport you in secret to Creech Air Force Base where you will pick up an SUV to drive into California. You will drive to Mammoth Lakes California. Leon is already set up there in a make-shift command center. You will meet him at the gas station on the corner of Main street and Mammoth road on the left. You'll be given all of this information plus a secure cell phone once you reach Creech."

"When am I flying out?" asks Doyle.

Aaron looks at his watch, "In about seventy-five minutes."

Doyle looks at him, "What? Tonight? I need to let Susan know."

Aaron pats him on the back, "She already knows. I sent two guys down there to inform her and remain there for her protection. We also have one person monitoring your parents as well while you're gone."

"Okay. Wow, you covered all the bases," Doyle replies.

"Doyle, after you park in the short-term parking lot proceed to the car rental area. Near the restrooms is an area for charging cell phones, take a seat and one of my guys will meet you there," explains Aaron.

"Got it," Doyle tells him.

"Be safe and I might see you out there next week. I have to fly overseas to check on another operation first," Aaron says as he shakes Doyle's hand.

Doyle shakes his hand, "Okay brother, you be safe too." He stands there and watches Aaron walk off into the darkness before he climbs

into his truck and drives off…

After having parked in the short-term parking area he walks into the car rental wing of the McGhee-Tyson airport.

Okay, there is the phone charging tables, he thinks as he starts walking towards them. *No one is around the area*; he thinks as he drops his travel bag and takes a seat.

He takes a small strap out of his bag and ties it around his luggage then to the leg of the chair, removes a small lock from his pocket and locks it to the strap. He walks into the restroom and enters one of the urinal stalls. As he is standing there a man in janitors overalls walks in and into the stall beside him.

"Don't say a word. After you wash your hands, leave your truck keys on the counter then exit, grab your gear, and head to your terminal," the man says to him.

Doyle just nods, zips his pants up and walks over and begins washing his hands. He dries his hands off then reaches in his pocket and pulls the truck keys out. He looks over at the man, who is staring at the wall.

"Time's wasting," the man says.

Doyle lays the keys down and walks out of the bathroom.

"Good evening, sir," the woman with the airport enforcement authority says.

"Good evening, ma'am," Doyle replies.

"I'll need you to take off your shoes, belt, and hat. Also place any laptops, phones, or other electronic devices in one of the boxes. Your shoes and all can go in another box, then place them on the conveyor to be screened," she explains to him.

"Step this way, sir," another security agent tells him. "Step into the metal detector, place your feet on the templates on the floor and hold your arms out," he explains to Doyle.

Sitting on a bench after getting dressed, Doyle looks through the envelope that Aaron gave him.

There is a note inside that reads: *Doyle, there is a supply store at Creech AFB, where you can get all the supplies you need. Thanks, Aaron.*

He puts the note in his shirt pocket and gets up to head towards the gate. As he reaches the gate, he notices that they have just started to board, *perfect timing,* he thinks.

"Sir. Welcome to the red-eye to Las Vegas," the attendant in first class says to Doyle.

"Thank you," he replies.

After takeoff and the plane has reached the cruising altitude, the attendant asks him, "It was a smooth take-off, don't you think? Would you like something to drink?"

"Yes, ma'am it was. Just water please," Doyle says with a smile.

"Alrighty. Here you go sweetie," she says handing him the water

bottle.

Doyle looks out of the window for a few minutes then pulls his hat down over his eyes and drifts off to sleep.

1322 HOURS
SEPTEMBER 11, 2001
IDAHO FALLS REGIONAL AIRPORT

"Dammit! All the lines are down in New York City," Doyle yells as he slams the payphone down into its holder, he stands there thinking.

"I'll just rent a damn car and drive my ass back home," he says out loud as he starts walking to the car rental area.

"More than one way to skin a cat!" he yells over at the airline ticket counter.

"Sir, I'm deeply sorry. The FAA has ordered all flights grounded," the ticket agent yells back to him.

Doyle walks up to the car rental counter, "Yes, I was going to drop off my rental this afternoon but instead I need to change up my rental agreement. I'm going to have to drive it back to New Jersey with the airlines shut down."

The agent types on the computer keypad, "I understand, sir. Give me just a minute to make the changes, there's fresh coffee in the lounge area."

Doyle walks over and pours a cup of coffee then he notices the tv

mounted on the wall is showing replays of the World Trade Center building one and two collapsing.

"This has to be terrorism," he says out loud.

The screen now switches to the overhead view of the Pentagon. Black smoke pours out of the hole in the side, "We truly are under attack," he whispers.

An older gentleman walks up beside Doyle, "This was an inside job son."

Doyle looks at him and asks, "What did you just say?"

The old man smiles, "You heard me you jackass, your people did this!"

Doyle sits his backpack down and walks over to the old man, "What the hell did you say?"

The agent at the car rental counter finishes with his rental agreement papers, "Sir. Mr. Anderson. Sir!"

Doyle now right in the face of the old man notices that it is colonel Miller, "What's going on?" he whispers.

The agent has now walked over and started to tug on Doyle's sleeve, "Sir. Sir."

Doyle jerks and looks up...

"Sir. You need to put your chair back in the upright position. We're preparing to land in Vegas," the flight attendant tells him.

"Yes, ma'am," he whispers. He looks out the window and sees the

lights of Vegas below as he wipes the sweat off his forehead. *That was a quick flight,* he thinks as he looks around the first-class area.

The moonlight is shining on the mountains off to the west and he can see the white caps on top of them.

"Why would Amy Leek be doing a wildfire study in the middle of winter?" he asks himself out loud.

He leans back in his chair as the plane drops and turns towards the runway, "Another shit-show I'm sure," he says.

He pulls his phone out of his pocket, "No messages...yet," he whispers.

0002 HOURS
PRESENT-DAY
MCCARRAN INTERNATIONAL AIRPORT, LAS VEGAS

Doyle reaches down and grabs his duffle bag off the luggage conveyor, "Now who am I supposed to look for?" he says looking around the area.

He walks out the exit where several taxis and ubers sit waiting when he hears, "Mr. Anderson?" a man standing by a car asks.

"Yes. That is me," he replies.

The man shows him his identification, "I'm to take you to the Bellagio Hotel and Casino for the seminar," the man tells him.

"Yes, that's correct. The SARs seminar, yes," Doyle says.

The man opens the trunk and takes Doyle's bag, "Mr. Anderson, sir. Let me open the back door for you."

Doyle looks at him, "Thank you. You don't have to call me sir," he says as he climbs into the car.

The man runs around the car and jumps in, "This your first time to Vegas Mr. Anderson?"

"No. But it's been fifteen years or so since I was here last," Doyle replies.

"A lot has changed since then Mr. Anderson," he says as they drive off. "We have the Golden Knights and the Raiders now Mr. Anderson," he says to Doyle.

"Yes, I heard that," Doyle replies looking out the window.

As they turn onto Las Vegas Blvd Doyle notices how much the city has built up in the past several years. "The city has really grown."

"Yes, Mr. Anderson. We are doing incredibly good," the driver replies as he looks at him in the rear-view mirror.

The sidewalks are crowded with people, "It's pretty cold for this many people to be out at this time of night," Doyle says as he looks around.

"Yes, it is Mr. Anderson. There were several special shows tonight since it's Super Bowl week," responds the driver.

"Oh, that's right. I forgot all about that," Doyle replies looking at his watch.

They pull up to the check-in drop at the Bellagio, the driver jumps out and opens the door for Doyle. "I hope you have a great stay Mr. Anderson," he says as he opens the trunk and hands Doyle his bag.

"Thank you. I'm sure I will," replies Doyle as he hands the driver a twenty-dollar bill.

As Doyle starts to walk away the driver says, "Oh...Mr. Anderson, be careful about what you search for. Never know what you'll find." Doyle stands there looking at him when the driver smiles, "Good night, Mr. Anderson." The driver runs around the car, jumps in, and speeds off.

"Okay. That was a little strange," Doyle says walking away…

"Here you go sir, third floor," the lady at the counter tells him.

"Thank you," replies Doyle as he turns to walk to the elevator.

"What floor?" the man in the elevator asks Doyle.

"Three, please," Doyle replies looking at the man and the woman with him.

"Two-hundred bucks is a steal for you tonight sweetie," the man tells the woman.

Doyle tries not to smile as the elevator stops at floor three. "Y'all have a good night," he tells them as he walks out of the elevator.

"You better believe we will!" the man yells as the doors close. Doyle shakes his head and walks down the hall to his room.

Doyle opens the door and walks in the room sitting his bag on the bed. Before he can sit down the phone rings.

"In the bathroom you will find a new set of clothes with a wig and glasses. After you have put them on, come down the stairs to the casino. From there, exit outside to the overhead crosswalk to Caesars Palace. Once on the other side veer to the right and use the Las Vegas Blvd overpass to cross over to the other side of the street. Walk north and enter the Flamingo Hotel on the right. Walk through the hotel and exit on the east side at the Flamingo & Caesars Palace bus station. One of my guys will pick you up there. Most importantly, leave your phone, clothes you have on now, and room key on the bed."

The call disconnects then Doyle hangs up, looks around and then begins to undress.

He walks into the bathroom, "Oh my God!"

Doyle stands there in shock. Hanging from the shower curtain rod is a white Elvis jumpsuit with an Elvis wig and glasses stuffed in the cummerbund. As he grabs the jumpsuit, he sees a note attached to it, "Wish I was there to see you wearing this...Leon."

Doyle laughs, "I'm going to kick his ass."

He undresses and slides the jump suit on. After he zips it up, he places the wig on his bald head, and grabs the glasses. "Thank you, thank you very much," he says looking in the mirror as he places the glasses on his face.

He walks down the hallway to the stairwell. Beside the door to the

stairs the walls are covered with mirrors, “Dear Lord,” he says as he sees his reflection.

As he enters the Casino one of the security guards’ yells to him, “I didn’t know Elvis had a beard!”

Doyle waves at the guard and says under his breath, “Eat another doughnut fat-man.”

Surprising to him, he blends in perfectly. Other than the guard no one pays any attention to him as he makes his way to the pickup point. As he exits the Flamingo near the bus stop a cop’s siren starts to blare and people scatter towards a scuffle by the pool.

Doyle stops and looks over at the fight when a man that was sitting on a bench nearby gets up and quickly walks towards him.

“Doyle, get in the red van it’s time we go,” the man tells him as he walks past.

“Okay, sure,” Doyle responds, opening the sliding door and throwing his bag in the back. He climbs in the front and the man pulls off, “We had to cause a little ruckus so that no one would notice us leaving,” the man tells him.

The man looks at him, “Nice to meet you finally Doyle. I’m Mike Rosen.”

Doyle shakes his hand, “Nice to meet you too.”

Mike drives between the Bellagio and Caesars then pulls onto interstate 15 then says, ‘I’m a retired Marine Sergeant Major. I worked for the SG for a little over six years then I flipped and now work for the

Patriots."

Doyle looks at him and asks, "Is that a fact?"

Mike smiles, "Yeah. Unfortunately, it is. I mainly worked in selling weapons to hostile regimes. But after Benghazi went down and guys were hung out to dry...I decided I was on the wrong side of history."

Doyle starts to remove the Elvis wig.

"Leave that on until we get to Creech Air Force Base," Mike tells him.

"The damn thing is hot," Doyle replies.

"I'm sure it is but we can't risk you being seen. They already have a hit out on me and I'm sure you'll be on that list very soon," says Mike as he checks his mirrors for tails.

"So, tell me more on why you joined the SG?" Doyle asks.

"We'll have plenty of time for that later. I'm your guide to get you up into Yosemite," replies Mike.

"Guide? Why do I need a guide?" asks Doyle.

Mike looks at him, "Yosemite is an extremely dangerous place. Do you know how many people have disappeared there and never been found?" Mike asks him.

"I have a very good idea," Doyle snaps.

"I'm afraid you don't. But you do not have a say in it. The only way you are going up in those mountains is with me, so get over it," Mike snaps back.

The two guys do not say anything else to each other until they are out of the city and into the desert.

"Besides, you'll be glad I'm with you once we find Jonah," Mike says.

"Why is that?" Doyle asks.

"You'll find out. I'll just say he's a handful."

Doyle sits there a few seconds, "Everyone keeps saying that."

Mike laughs and sets the cruise control, "We'll be there in about thirty minutes, then you can get out of those silly clothes. Leon wanted me to take your picture, but I didn't want you to break my phone if I did."

Doyle laughs, "I wouldn't have broken it, but I may have stuffed it up Leon's butt!"

The two guys laugh as they drive off into the dark desert.

The stars shine bright over the desolate landscape.

Chapter Three:
GAME PLAN

0300 HOURS
PRESENT-DAY
CREECH AIR FORCE BASE, NEVADA

"There's a few things you should know before we pull into Creech," Mike tells Doyle as he slows down to turn towards the main entrance to Creech Air Force Base.

"Yeah. What's that?" Doyle asks.

Mike looks at him, "For starters, I give the orders, I don't take orders. If I tell you to do something you better damn-well do it. I spent my whole life fighting for this country, so I don't have to prove anything to you."

"I never asked you to," replies Doyle.

"Don't interrupt me. I have seen guys come and go from our Patriots group that thought they were hot stuff; they did not last a week before they got killed. This is not the military; you do not get discharged if you don't cut the mustard here. You die."

"Understood," Doyle replies.

"Now put your glasses back on we're coming up on the gate," Mike tells him.

As they pull to the gate, the guard motions for them to stop.

"How are we doing tonight, sir?" the guard asks.

"We're doing really well," Mike replies, handing him his badge.

"What's up with your friend?" asks the guard.

"He's on temporary duty travel from Edwards Air Force base and he does Elvis impersonations on the Vegas strip," Mike tells him as he hands the guard Doyle's fake ids.

The guard looks over both badges, "Okay gentlemen, you two have a good night. You may proceed," he tells them, handing the badges back to them.

"Thank you, goodnight," Mike says as he drives through the gate.

"Elvis impersonations? Really?" asks Doyle.

"How else was I going to explain the outfit?" Mike asks laughing.

He drives past the runway and around the main part of the base then heads north out into wide-open desert.

"The stars are really bright out here, uh?" Mike asks.

"Yes, they are," Doyle replies.

They drive for a few miles until the blacktop turns into sand then they turn right through a gate into a vehicle storage area. Large

combat military vehicles sit in endless rows along the flat desert plain. Mike drives to the back of the lot where an office trailer sits against the yard's fence.

"Let's go, Elvis," Mike tells him as he gets out of the van.

"Listen, jackass," Doyle replies.

Mike opens the door to the trailer and walks in, "Gentlemen. This is Doyle Anderson."

Doyle walks in behind him and the two guys in the trailer start laughing. "Laugh it up, guys," he says as both the men come over to shake his hand.

"It's very good to meet you, Anderson," one of the men tells him.

"Yes, we've heard a lot about you," the other man says.

"Thanks, guys," Doyle replies, jerking the wig from his head. "Where is my change of clothes?" Doyle asks.

"Go through that door and everything you need is in there," Mike tells him.

Doyle emerges fifteen minutes later, dressed in jeans and a camouflaged button-up shirt.

"Now that looks better," says Mike.

"What about boots?" Doyle asks.

"Other end of the office. There are three types to choose from plus a dozen phones, just grab one," Mike explains to him.

One of the men walks over to a large gun safe and opens it,

"Choose anything you want out of here too."

"Doyle, we need to go over our game plan," Mike tells him.

"Sure, go ahead," replies Doyle.

"We're going to get some rest then at 0800 hours we are going to travel west through the desert by jeep. It will take us most of the day to reach Beatty, Nevada. Once we get near Beatty there is a vehicle hidden there for us," explains Mike.

"Why are we cutting through the desert?" Doyle asks.

"They are looking for us, Doyle. They think you are still in Vegas, but they know I am here. Cutting through the desert will hopefully buy us enough time to reach Jonah's position. I'm counting on two days at least," Mike tells him as he opens a map and lays it on a table nearby.

"Won't someone see us leaving here?" asks Doyle.

"These two guys are going to haul us out into the desert where we'll pick up the jeep. Once we are in Beatty, we will drive west on highway 374 into California and through Death Valley then up interstate 395 to Mammoth Lakes," Mike explains to him.

"Now, you better get some sleep Doyle. There's a cot in the room you got dressed in," Mike says as he walks to the opposite end of the office trailer.

"Sir, we'll stand guard," one of the men says to Mike.

"Sounds good. Doyle I'll see you at 0745 hours," Mike says as he

closes the door to a small room.

0745 HOURS
PRESENT-DAY
NORTH OF CREECH AIR FORCE BASE

Doyle walks outside where he sees Mike talking with the two men, "You finally up sleepy-head," Mike says to him.

"Yeah, I'm ready to go," replies Doyle.

Mike walks over to a Humvee and opens the back hatch, "Load your gear then get in, we have a long trip ahead of us."

One of the two men helping them starts the Humvee and pulls out of the lot. They drive north along the sand road until they come to a security post, the man driving waves at the guard and continues north for another five miles. They come to an intersection and turn left where they drive west until the sand road ends.

"This is as far as we go gentlemen," the driver says.

The two men jump out and walk over to a tarp covered vehicle, they pull the tarp off revealing a dune buggy.

"There's plenty of room for your gear in the back and there's four extra gallons of gasoline in the cans on the side rack," the driver tells them.

"That's no jeep," Doyle tells Mike.

"Yeah, it's better than a jeep," replies Mike with a grin on his face.

"We won't be able to move in the morning after riding in that all day," Doyle says walking over and checking the suspension on the dune buggy.

"You'll be okay sweetie, I'm seventy-three and I'm not worried about it," Mike tells him.

Doyle just shakes his head, "This will not be fun."

Mike rolls his eyes and walks around to the other side of the dune buggy.

"Okay. Gentlemen, that's all of your gear, we've got to go before we draw anyone's attention," one of the men tells Mike and Doyle.

The men climb into the Humvee and drive off.

"Well, get in Doyle," Mike says.

"Have you ever driven one of these?" Doyle asks him.

"I used to race these back in the day, so yeah." Mike pauses then continues, "We're going to go south about a mile then we'll cut through the mountains in a dried creek bed."

"Back in the day? What, like 1930?" Doyle asks.

"Don't be a smart-ass Doyle, just get in."

"Alright then, let's go, just don't crash and kill us," Doyle says laughing.

Mike starts the dune buggy and throws sand fifteen feet up in the air as he takes off. "You better hang on," he tells him with a huge grin on his face…

As they reach the dried creek Mike looks at him, "Keep an eye out for anyone. There's a few sections coming up where the cliff walls are right on top of us."

Doyle looks up at the mountains as they enter the creek bed, "Why didn't we just take the highway?" he asks.

"Like I have been trying to tell you, they know I am here, so the SG is on high alert. Every vehicle leaving Creech will be monitored or even followed," explains Mike.

"Where do you normally work?" Doyle asks.

"California. But I go wherever I am needed, but every time I leave the state of California, they try to kill me," Mike tells him as he leans out of the dune buggy looking up for anyone.

"What about those guys at the security post as we left Creech?" asks Doyle.

"They're with us," Mike says as they hit a large bump.

"You said every time you leave California, so they won't try and kill you in California?" Doyle asks.

Mike looks at him, "I wouldn't say they won't but it's not as likely."

Doyle keeps watching the cliffs until they come to a large, dried lakebed, "Isn't this an old nuclear test site?"

Mike nods his head, "Yes, it is. Frenchman Flat or Frenchman Lake," Mike tells him.

"Are we allowed out here?" Doyle asks, sounding concerned.

"We are today. That is why we came this way, a little extra protection," explains Mike.

Mike speeds up kicking a cloud of dust into the air as he races across the dried lakebed. "We should make better time now," he yells to Doyle over the dune buggies engine noise. They travel just south of the remains from the old nuclear testing site then crossover several blacktop roads. Mike stops the dune buggy just before they enter another dried creek bed.

"We better fuel up, so we don't have to stop while going through the tight areas," he says pointing ahead. "If you need to use the restroom or eat something now's the time, we've been traveling for about three hours now," Mike tells him.

"How much farther?" Doyle asks.

"About forty-two miles. Once we get through this valley, we will travel alongside Interstate 95 on dirt roads to Beatty," explains Mike.

After Mike fuels up, the two guys sit down in the shade from the dune buggy to eat lunch. "Good thing we're not making this trip in the summer when it's a hundred and ten degrees out here," Mike says.

"That's true," replies Doyle before asking. "What do you do for the Patriots?"

Mike takes a bite of his sandwich and takes a few chews, "I'm a fixer. You name it, I do it."

Doyle tosses several small rocks at an old soda can lying nearby,

"Ever think about retiring?" he asks.

"Nope. I'll die doing this," Mike replies, then points to the north.

"That's Skull Mountain."

"Interesting," Doyle says looking at the desolate mountain standing tall in the background.

"On the other side is what's known as Jackass Flats," Mike tells him.

"Oh. Your hometown uh?" Doyle says laughing.

"That's right. We better get going in case we run into trouble," Mike says getting to his feet.

"Okay," Doyle replies.

They climb back into the dune buggy and Mike starts it up, "Same thing as before, keep an eye on the cliffs."

Doyle grabs onto the door as Mike takes off, "I got it covered," he says.

About an hour later they exit the valley and Doyle notices another dune buggy coming towards them from the north. "We've got company Mike!" he yells.

Mike looks over at the dune buggy racing towards them, "Hang on!"

He presses the pedal to the floor and pulls away from the approaching buggy. They come off the ground a few times as Mike maneuvers towards a narrow dirt road. He hits the brakes causing them to slide sideways up and onto the road before he floors the pedal again.

"You still see them?" he yells to Doyle.

Doyle looks back trying to catch a glimpse of the other buggy through all the dust kicked in the air. "Mike, I don't see them, looks like they went the opposite direction."

Mike looks in his mirrors then says, "That's a good thing."

They continue on the dirt road when Mike looks at Doyle, "We're passing behind a gas station and a world-famous alien gift center. You want me to stop so you can buy an Area 51 tee shirt?" Mike asks laughing.

"No, I'm good," replies Doyle.

The two guys travel alongside the interstate for thirty more miles when Mike pulls over, "We need fuel." He shuts the engine off and they both climb out.

"I've eaten enough dust I won't need any super," Doyle says, rinsing his mouth out with water then spitting.

"We've only got about six miles to go. Don't get too comfortable, we're sitting ducks out here." Mike tells him.

After Mike adds the remaining fuel, he quickly gets back in the dune buggy, "Let's go Doyle."

Doyle jogs back to the buggy and climbs in, "Ready."

"What was you doing over there?" asks Mike.

Doyle smiles, "Just watching traffic on the highway."

"You are one strange cat," Mike says as he starts the buggy and takes

off.

As they get to the outskirts of Beatty, they come up on a trailer park on their left and few homesteads on the right. Mike pulls into the driveway of one of the homesteads and parks behind a barn. Another vehicle sits there covered, “Help me remove this tarp,” Mike tells him.

“It’s a Death Valley National Park service vehicle,” Doyle says after they uncover the SUV.

“Perfect way to blend in driving through Death Valley, don’t you think? Now let’s get our gear and cover the dune buggy,” Mike says.

Mike grabs a small briefcase out of the back seat of the SUV, “Here, put this necklace on,” he says handing Doyle a small box.

“What’s this?” Doyle asks.

“That device is for your protection and must be worn at all times. It will beep if one of those SG suits gets within one-hundred yards of you,” explains Mike.

“Really?” asks Doyle as he puts it around his neck.

“One very important thing, you lose this, and I will personally shoot you between the eyes,” Mike says looking directly at him.

“We’re leaving our protected area, so we’ll need these,” says Mike.

“What do you mean protected area?” Doyle asks.

“We were close enough to government property where they were scanning the area for us. Now we are on our own,” Mike tells him as he climbs into the SUV.

Doyle climbs in and Mike reaches in the glove box then continues, "This clip is for your 9mm, you keep this on you at all times. This is only to be used against the suit...do you understand?" Mike asks.

"Yes," replies Doyle.

"Do not shoot these bullets at anything but the suit, if you do…"

Doyle cuts him off, "Yeah, I know, you'll shoot me between the eyes."

Mike drops the clip into Doyle's lap, "Damn straight I will."

Mike starts the SUV and slowly drives back down the driveway, "We know for a fact that the SG has only one suit in operation. Thanks to your buddy the other one is out of commission for several more months."

Doyle looks at him, "How do you know it'll take several more months?" he asks.

"We intercepted the shipment with the repair parts, it'll take that long for the vendor to make new ones," explains Mike. "What we don't know is if they'll use their one working suit to try and stop us from reaching Jonah or just go after him," Mike tells him as he pulls out onto the highway.

"Do we know where Jonah is?" Doyle asks.

"We know the area but not the exact location, that's what you're for, the mountain expert," Mike says looking at him.

"He won't stand a chance against that suit," Doyle replies.

Mike pulls up to a traffic light, "He helped design those suits Doyle."

Doyle quickly turns and looks at Mike, "Say what? Hold on a damn second, there is way too much you have not told me. He helped design the suits. What kind of crap is that?" demands Doyle.

Mike continues on as the light turns green, "Doyle, you should have known with all your military background. You're on a need-to-know basis."

Doyle turns and reaches in the back and pulls a cigar out of his pack, "That's bull crap!" he snaps.

Mike looks at him, "Don't light that in here."

Doyle sticks the cigar in his mouth and lights it, "You'll be alright," he says with the cigar between his lips.

"At least roll your window down," Mike snaps.

Doyle lowers his window, and the two guys sit in silence as they drive down highway 374 towards Death Valley.

Doyle tosses the cigar butt out the window just before the go through Hells Gate into Death Valley National Park.

"I'm glad you're done with that stinking thing," Mike says to him.

"You keep information from me, and I'll keep smoking them in here, you be straight with me then I'll wait until we stop," Doyle replies.

They continue through Death Valley for the next forty-five minutes

without any problems. As they reach interstate 395 Mike says, "We take this north to Mammoth Lakes."

"When you said Jonah helped design the suit, how can that be if the SG uses the older version?" Doyle asks.

"He helped design the new software that controls the suits, both for the SGs version and the newer version," replies Mike.

"Do you know much about the suit software?" asks Doyle.

"Nope. All I know is it's connected to the operator's nervous system somehow." Mike tells him.

Doyle takes in the information then asks, "These gadgets around our necks. You know much about these?"

Mike looks at him, "What's up with all the questions? No, I don't know much about these, but I do know it would be easier to get the nuclear codes than get your hands on one of these."

"Seems like you got them easy enough," Doyle says under his breathe.

"Excuse me?" Mike asks slowing down.

Doyle turns and looks out the window, "Oh, nothing."

"Why do we have to wear them around our necks?" asks Doyle.

"We don't have too, it's just harder to lose them this way. Now shut the hell up we will be there soon," snaps Mike as he turns the radio on.

1700 HOURS
PRESENT-DAY
MAMMOTH LAKES, CALIFORNIA

Mike turns left off Main street onto Old Mammoth road, "We should see him pull out of the gas station right about now."

After Mike says that an old Chevy pick-up truck pulls out in front of them and taps it's brakes twice.

"That's him," Mike tells Doyle.

They drive past the Snow creek golf course and continue until the road is blocked by a huge sign that reads 'closed for winter'. They drive around the sign and pull into a gravel drive that leads to one of the city's water tanks. Two men swing open a gate and both vehicles pull in and park in front of an office trailer.

"It's about time you guys showed up!" Leon yells from the porch of the office trailer. "Now come on in, it's cold out here," Leon says as he walks back into the trailer.

Mike and Doyle grab their gear and walk into the trailer, "This is not what I was expecting," Doyle says.

"Yeah, we're disguised as construction workers," Leon says before slapping him on the arm.

"How are you Doyle?" he asks.

"I'm good Leon, you?"

Leon walks over and shakes Mike's hand, "Oh, I can't complain

Doyle."

Doyle looks out the window and sees men removing the Death Valley decals and license plates from the SUV.

"They'll get it ready for you guys in no time," Leon explains to them.

Mike walks over and sits down on a small couch, "You might want to explain to Doyle what the game plan is...he tends to ask a lot of questions."

Leon sits down, "Yes, I will Mike. Doyle, please sit down, take a load off," Leon tells him.

After Doyle sits down Leon continues, "Our last hit on Jonah was in the Sierra National Forest near Lake Thomas A Edison. He is bunkered down in that area with his device he made that keeps anyone in one of those suits from getting too close to him."

Doyle asks, "What do you mean a device?"

Leon hands Doyle a sheet of paper with a drawing of the device, "It sends out a signal that disables the suit. In other words, the invisibility is gone and the ability to fly as well." Leon pauses then continues, "Jonah has the only one, since he built the software, he knows how to shut it down. Hopefully, we can reach him before they do since we're going in on foot."

"It will take us days from here on foot," Doyle says.

"That's true and it'll take eight hours by car and then you still have to hike in," Leon explains. "So... that leaves us with only one option,

fly you two up the mountain," Leon says with a soft laugh.

"That's the best way for sure," Doyle replies.

"Since we don't want to tip off Jonah that we're coming we'll drop you off near Mono Hot Springs. You'll have to go on foot the rest of the way," Leon tells Doyle.

"That shouldn't be a problem, I'll just need a good map of the area," replies Doyle.

Leon tosses him a small map, "There you are. Also, he might have moved up in elevation near Devil's Bathtub, a small lake below Graveyard Peak."

Doyle looks at him, "I don't like the names of those places. The natives always named bad places with names like that," Doyle says looking at Mike.

"As soon as it gets good and dark, we'll take you guys to our helicopter and fly you in. I'd spend the next few hours getting your gear ready, we have everything you might need in the back room," explains Leon.

Mike leans his head against the back of the couch and closes his eyes, "Doyle, you're in charge of getting our gear together. I'm going to take a nap," he tells him.

Leon types on the keyboard of his computer, "Look here Doyle, there's hardly any snow on the ground up there. Been a bad year for skiers," Leon says.

"Well, that's a good thing. Snow can really slow you down," Doyle

replies.

Leon looks up at Doyle, "Now listen to me, this Jonah cat, he's a little whacked in the head. I mean, he is not all there. He's looking for a war against the SG so, be careful."

"Why does he want a war with them?" Doyle asks.

"He thinks they screwed him over on the payment for his software plus his sister is missing. He thinks we are in man's last days. He talks nonstop, that is, if he lets you two get close to him," Leon explains.

"Are we protecting him or bringing him back down the mountain?" asks Doyle.

"First thing is to find him, then we'll assess things from there," says Leon.

Doyle sits there thinking about what Leon just said.

Mike starts to snore.

A cold wind blows down from the mountain.

Chapter Four: CORNSTALK

1912 HOURS
PRESENT-DAY
CONSTRUCTION TRAILER IN MAMMOTH LAKES, CALIFORNIA

"Mike is sleeping good," Leon says to Doyle as he walks through the door into the back office.

"Let him sleep. I've got all the gear I think we'll need loaded up in the SUV," replies Doyle sitting with his feet propped up on a desk and his hat pulled over his eyes.

Leon sits down in a chair beside the desk, "You know, Mike volunteered to come pick you up. He said he wanted to meet the man that saved that family in South Africa."

Doyle adjusts his feet and replies in a soft voice, "I don't talk about that mission."

"I know but it won't hurt anything now. You're one of the last guys that's still alive that was on that mission," Leon tells him. "So, tell me

about how you saved that family at the very least," he says to him.

Doyle sits there a few minutes then speaks, "I can't tell you why we were there but, we had orders to take out a certain individual. Navy Seals had come in from a submarine to help us."

Doyle yawns then continues, "We came in up a small river from an undisclosed location. We met the Seals at 0400, then we hid our boat about a mile and a half from the compound where our subject was located."

Leon nods his head, "The good old Seals. What team?" he asks Doyle.

"I can't tell you that but, they have all since been killed in action. Anyway, we ran into a few guards on our way to the compound. We took them out like taking candy from a baby."

"They probably never knew what hit them," Leon says laughing.

"No, they never had a chance. You kind of feel sorry for them looking back on it now, they had no idea that that day was going to be their last. But when you hang with those types of people you get what you ask for."

Doyle sits in silence for a few minutes before continuing, "We broke into two groups and breached the fence in seconds, encountering another few sitting ducks. We knew what part of the compound our target was bed down in and we figured he only had women with him. Now up to this point we have not made a sound, no one knew we were inside the compound."

“That’s how good you guys were,” Leon says.

“We were great, not just good,” Doyle replies then pauses before continuing. “The Seals went to our target and my crew kept watch and made sure our exit remained clear. Absolutely no one was moving around inside, everyone was sleeping. We heard four suppressed gun shots and in a blink of an eye the Seals were standing in front of us. So, we shagged, and were out of the compound in seconds.”

“No one even knew y’all were there,” says Leon.

“Well, something happened, or someone saw us. After we cleared the fence and was almost to the tree line the entire complex caught on fire, not sure how but it did. Not just one building, the whole damn place. Almost like we triggered something, or someone did see us. That’s when I heard a woman screaming that her kids were trapped.”

Doyle pauses, “I don’t know why to this day...but something made me turn around and go help those kids. It is against everything we are trained to do; we completed our mission, and I should have been gone. I told the rest of the group to go and that I would meet them at the rendezvous point soon. I also told them that If I wasn’t there in fifteen minutes to leave without me.”

Leon hangs on every word as Doyle continues. “I jumped the fence and ran over to the room they were trapped in. This complex looked like apartment buildings with the room doors facing outside. Now this whole place was engulfed in flames, I could hear the kids screaming in terror…”

Doyle drops his feet off the desk and sits up, looking down at the floor he continues, "I tried to kick the door in, but it wouldn't budge. Someone had blocked it shut so that the kids could not get out. I ran around to the back of the building and saw a window air conditioning unit in the wall, not in a window just in the wall. I tore that damn thing apart and pushed it into the building as smoke poured out of the hole, I tied my shirt around my face and climbed in.

Luckily, I found the kids in the next room, two little girls lying beside their little brother who'd already passed out from the smoke."

"I picked the boy up and motioned for the girls to follow me on their hands and knees. We crawled to the hole where I passed the boy out to his mom and then the little girls crawled out. You must keep in mind that we just killed a high value target and that his men are looking for us. After I crawled out, I performed CPR on the boy the whole-time hearing gunshots and men yelling. I was able to revive him, then told the woman I had to go now."

Leon, now sitting there with his hand over his mouth says, "My goodness, that's awesome, brother."

Doyle looks up at him, "Yeah, but now I'm trapped inside the compound. As I start looking for how I am going to escape, one of the little girls whispers something in her mom's ear. The mom tells me there is a tunnel nearby that leads out of the compound and into the forest."

"Oh wow!" Leon exclaims.

"They lead me over to it and both the little girls jump in to show me the way. It was a drainage pipe that had several paths leading different directions that was easy to get turned around in. The woman said they all were coming with me and that they would be killed if they stayed behind. I tried to talk her out of it but didn't have time, so we all climbed in the pipe with her holding the little boy," Doyle explains as he stands up and walks over to the window.

"The pipe was big enough for me to crawl in on my belly, but I couldn't get up on my knees to crawl," Doyle tells him then continues. "This thing smelled like shit and it went on forever with several turns, I could hear men yelling looking for me and my guys above us. The pipe led us to a small creek inside the tree line, after the girls climbed out, I climbed out and scanned the area. I radioed my guys and told them I had four packages with me."

"We were about two miles from the rendezvous point but in the opposite direction that I needed to go. The guys said they would backtrack to our location to provide cover for us. I could hear men running towards us, so I told the mother and the kids to get back into the pipe. I set up a position just above the drainage pipe and one by one I dropped all four of the guys heading our way.

After I got them out of the pipe it took us forty-five minutes to safely reach the boat and get out of there. We found out later that the lady and her kids had been trafficked and was being held in that location. We also found out later that many other mothers and their children died in that fire. If we knew what that place was, we would

have killed every son-of-a-bitch there and saved every woman and child," Doyle says now looking at Leon.

"I know, but how could you have known?" Leon asks.

"Somebody damn well knew!" Doyle snaps. "That is the thing, they send you out on a mission and never give you all the details. Hell, someone in the United States might have been running that place, some Hollywood big shot," Doyle says. "We could have saved all of them."

"I know you could have. Did you ever hear what happened to the family you saved?" asks Leon. "Yeah, they moved them to Cleveland, Ohio. I heard later that all three of the children had graduated from college," replies Doyle.

"That's great man," Leon says.

"You know, I think back on that mission and I feel like we were set up. There was no one up, no one heard us. Then the whole damn thing catches fire...how is that?" Doyle asks looking at Leon.

"Brother, I don't know," answers Leon.

Mike opens the door, "What are you ladies doing in here?"

Leon laughs, "Just talking about old times."

"Don't you think we should be going?" Mike asks.

"Yeah. I'm ready when you guys are," Leon tells him. Mike closes the door then Leon looks at Doyle, "He's a grumpy old man, don't take anything he says to heart."

Doyle smiles, "He's no problem, I've dealt with tougher guys before. That is the first time I have ever spoken about 'Cornstalk', do not repeat a word of it," he tells Leon.

"No problem Doyle. It was probably good you talked about it," Leon tells him.

"Listen Doyle, about Mike...you do know he worked with the SG for a while, right?" Leon asks.

"Yeah, he told me. Selling weapons or something," replies Doyle.

"That's correct. He is a weapons genius. Now, he never participated in any murders or anything like that, he just helped arm groups fighting for freedom, at least that is what he thought. He realized what was going on after the Benghazi attack," Leon explains to him.

"Benghazi...I'd love to get my hands on the people that hung them out to dry!" snapped Doyle.

"Mike was working there with the Ambassador; he had flown to Qatar with a shipment when the attack happened. He wasn't supposed to fly to Qatar but the guy that was to go had gotten sick, so Mike took his spot," explains Leon.

"He was so upset about the attack that he flew to Washington and tried to get in to see the head of the CIA at the time. He was going to beat him to death, but he was arrested and spent a few months behind bars until we got him out," Leon tells him.

"Wow. I wish he would have beat him to death," Doyle says laughing.

“Yeah. I would never bring up that man’s name to him, unless you want to fight,” Leon replies.

“One other thing, those bullets in that clip he gave you for the suit, he came up with that technology,” Leon tells him as they both walk out of the room.

“Really?” asks Doyle.

“Really, what?” Mike asks.

“Oh, nothing,” Leon says to Mike.

“You two are like two little chatty girls,” Mike tells them.

“Mike, everything is loaded up in the SUV. I put a one-man tent in each of our backpacks as well,” Doyle tells him.

Mike looks at Doyle, “Good thinking.”

Leon sits down at the computer, “Look guys, using those devices you’re wearing around your necks I’ll be able to track your movements. Also, anytime Jonah uses his device it’ll ping on here as well.”

Doyle leaning over looking at the computer screen asks, “Has he used it?”

“O’yeah, several times. I am not sure if the SG has an operator in a suit up there or if he is just freaking out. His last known position was here,” Leon says pointing at the location on the monitor.

“You will update us if it pings again, correct?” Mike asks.

“Yes Mike, I’ll let you know immediately. Better yet, hand me your phones and I will sync them with this program, that way you will

receive the ping and have access to a real time map," Leon explains to them.

"That's much better," replies Mike.

"It's too bad we couldn't track the suits the same way," Doyle says.

"We can for a short time. But the software updates every few minutes and only Jonah knows the algorithm of how it updates," Leon tells them.

"That's why they want him, he programmed it in a way that it's impossible to figure out," Mike says.

"That's correct Mike. So, in other words Doyle it is impossible to track the suits," explains Leon.

"Then how do these things track them?" Doyle asks holding onto the device on the necklace.

"They don't track the suit; they just detect them when they get within range. But do not ask me what they detect, that too was designed by Jonah," says Leon.

Leon unhooks their phones from the computer, "Okay guys, you're all set. Y'all ready to drive to the chopper?" he asks.

"Yes, we're ready," Mike replies.

"Alrighty then, one of my men will take you guys out to the airport where we have an MH-6 Little Bird standing by," Leon tells them.

"That's the small one right," Mike asks.

Doyle walks up to Mike and places his hand on his shoulder,

"That's right, you're in my world now."

They walk outside where one of the men has already started the SUV, so it will be warm for them. "Call me as soon as you're on the ground so I can get your location on the computer," Leon tells Doyle.

"Will do brother," Doyle replies.

"Be safe guys," Leon says then turns and walks back into the trailer.

"You ready?" Mike asks Doyle.

"Yes, sir. Let us do this," says Doyle as he climbs in the SUV. The other men open the gate, and they drive out and back onto the snow-covered road.

"I take it you don't like flying?" Doyle asks Mike.

"I'm not crazy about it, especially in a helicopter," Mike replies.

"This little bird is a bad momma-jamma…fast," Doyle says.

"I can't wait," responds Mike.

"So, you like fast dune buggies but not fast helicopters uh?" asks Doyle.

"If you must know, I have an inner ear condition. Flying makes me dizzy," replies Mike.

"Oh, okay. I'll ask the pilot to fly smoothly," Doyle says with a grin on his face.

Mike sits there a few seconds then says, "The shooting you between the eyes looks better all the time."

Doyle laughs, "Well, I hate to tell you, but...you'll need to get in line."

"I can imagine that line is very long," Mike says, turning to look out the window.

"Oh, it is. Exceptionally long," Doyle whispers to himself.

2100 HOURS
PRESENT-DAY
MAMMOTH YOSEMITE AIRPORT

The SUV pulls off the interstate and onto Hot Creek Hatchery Road then right onto Airport Road. They continue and turn right and up to a gate; two men walk out and open the gate then motion for the SUV to proceed. They drive between two buildings and stop near the end of them, "Okay guys, this is as far as we go," the driver says.

"Roger-that," Doyle replies, opening the door. He walks around to the back and pulls both his and Mike's backpack out.

"Here you go Mike," he says.

"Thank you," Mike replies.

Doyle closes the back hatch, and the SUV drives off. They can hear the helicopter running and as they walk out from behind the building. "Fine machine," Doyle says as they see the small helicopter.

"Good evening gentlemen," the copilot says to them.

"Good evening," Mike replies.

"Watch your head as you climb aboard," the copilot tells them.

After they climb in the back the copilot hands each of them a set of headphones, "Please put these on gentlemen."

"Good evening guys, glad to be a service to you both," the pilot says. "There's a front moving in so this may be a bumpy ride. We are going to fly north a bit so we can fly through a valley over Yosemite National Park. We'll fly at an altitude of approximately ten-thousand feet and then circle back to the south-east to your drop point," explains the pilot.

"Sounds good," replies Doyle as he pushes the mic closer to his mouth.

"Hopefully, your subject will not hear us coming in, I know he won't see us because we're going in dark," the pilot says. "We will not touch down but will only be a few feet off the ground. You guys drop out and down to your knees with your head towards the ground. I'll be gone in a flash and you guys can do your thing," explains the pilot.

The copilot checks to make sure they are strapped in then gives the pilot the thumbs up. The helicopter lifts off the ground facing south then swings back to the left and turns north, almost doing a backflip.

"Hell yeah! I love this shit!" Doyle shouts looking at Mike, who has a white-knuckle hold on the seat, staring out the window.

They fly over Mammoth Lakes then slightly turn to the west before entering Yosemite National Park air space. They encounter a lot of

turbulence that bounces the helicopter from side to side as the fly between two mountain peaks.

"Hang on Mike," Doyle says to him as they hit a dead pocket of air and the helicopter drops in altitude. Mike pulls his sock hat off and wipes the sweat from his bald head.

"Take deep breaths. In through the nose and out through the mouth," explains Doyle.

The snow really highlights the trees and rocks below making it look like a painting, "Beautiful isn't it?" Doyle says trying to keep Mike from thinking about being sick.

The helicopter banks hard to the left turning south to the drop zone. "Okay, guys get ready we'll be there in about a minute," the pilot says through the headset.

"Go ahead and open the side doors," the copilot tells them.

They both open the doors and then the copilot says, "Good job. Now hook on to the tether and slide out onto the bench with your feet on the skids."

They both hook on to the tether, "Mike you go first so I can help you," Doyle tells him. Mike turns facing outward and slides outside onto the bench then drops his feet down on the skids.

"Great job buddy!" Doyle shouts as he turns and slides out onto his bench on the opposite side of the helicopter.

The helicopter starts dropping in altitude and shuts all its lights off. The pilot looking through night vision goggles lines the helicopter up

with the drop zone.

"Guys, as soon as I say unhook, you unhook and drop out of the helicopter," the copilot explains.

The Helicopter slows down and drops to under twenty feet above the ground. "Okay guys, on my mark," the copilot says. As soon as the helicopter is under five feet from the ground the copilot yells, "Unhook!"

Mike and Doyle both unhook and drop out of the helicopter. Mike hits and drops to his knees and then onto his face. Doyle hits and drops to his knees and lowers his head down to the ground. The helicopter speeds off and is quickly out of sight.

"You okay, Mike?" Doyle asks.

"Yeah, I'm fine," Mike replies just before throwing up.

Doyle stands up, "My knees have done that too many times." He walks over to Mike and holds his hand out, "Let me help you up."

He helps Mike over to a large boulder nearby, "Here you go, sit here and rest and I'll let Leon know we're on the ground," Doyle tells him.

"Okay, thanks," replies Mike.

They both sit down on the boulder then Doyle pulls his phone out of his pocket, "Leon, we're on the ground," he tells him.

"Okay, great. I have your position marked and I should be able to track you guys from there," Leon says.

"Any more pings from Jonah?" Doyle asks.

"Yes, while you guys were in the air, I received a ping from his device. It is not great news, but it is what I expected. He has moved further up the mountain; he is now in the Devil's Bathtub lake area. I'd say he's set up camp there for the night," explains Leon.

"Just looking at the map, I doubt we can make it to his location before sunrise. So, I think we will find a good place to camp then at first light head that way," Doyle tells him.

"That sounds like a good plan Doyle. Hey, just to let you know, it looks like a surprise snowstorm might be heading your way. Keep that in mind when you choose your route to him. Also, I will send out an update to both of your phones so y'all will get the pings as well," Leon explains.

"Will do, brother. Talk to you soon, bye," says Doyle as he disconnects the phone call.

"Mike, when you feel up to it, we need to find a good place to set up camp for the night," Doyle says to him.

"Give me just a minute and I'll be ready," replies Mike.

Doyle, using his headlamp, studies the map as Mike drinks some water. "How long has this ear thing bothered you?" asks Doyle.

"A few years I guess," Mike says.

"Sucks getting old doesn't it?" Doyle asks him.

"If you're not getting older then you're dead," replies Mike.

"True that," says Doyle.

Doyle sits there looking up at the sky, "You wouldn't believe me if I told you how many times, I've hit the ground on a search and the weather turns bad. It's almost like mother nature doesn't like me," Doyle tells him.

"She probably thinks you talk way the hell too much...damn! Do you ever shut up?" Mike asks.

Doyle laughs and then answers, "Nope. And by the way, you're a grumpy old fart."

"That I am," Mike says laughing.

Doyle stands up, "You ready? We need to find a place and get our tents up before it starts snowing."

Mike stands up and pops his neck, "Yeah I'm ready."

The two men start heading up the mountain.

Jonah sits on a ledge looking down into the valley.

The snow starts to fall.

Chapter Five:
UP THE MOUNTAIN

2206 HOURS
PRESENT-DAY
NORTH OF MONO HOT SPRINGS, CALIFORNIA

"Mike, watch your step. With this snow falling it is hard to see the rocks on the ground. We don't need an injury to deal with in this weather," Doyle tells him after they had been walking for ten minutes since the drop. "We're almost to Tule Lake if you want, we can stop there and ride this storm out?" Doyle asks.

"You're the mountain expert," Mike replies.

Doyle laughs then responds, "We probably should so we don't get off track with the poor visibility."

They walk around the west side of the lake, "There's some large boulders," Doyle says, shining his flashlight. "We don't want to set our tents up under any trees in case a limb breaks off and falls," he explains. They find a level area on the south side of one of the large boulders. "That'll keep the wind and snow off of us," says Doyle

pointing to a location.

“There’s no way we’ll get a fire going in this. It has to be blowing at least forty miles per hour,” Mike tells him trying to keep his footing in the snow that is now piling up.

Doyle drops his pack, “Mike we need to get our tents up before it gets worse. Then I want you in your sleeping bag so you can retain your body heat.”

Mike drops his pack, “That’s the smartest thing you’ve said all night.”

“It’s 2315 hours, let’s rest until 0400 and hopefully the storm will pass by then so we can continue,” Doyle says looking at his watch.

“That sounds like a plan,” Mike replies, then climbs into his tent.

After Doyle is in his tent, he kicks off his boots then props his flashlight up like a lantern and studies his map. He makes several marks on it then looks at his phone to compare its map with his paper one. He turns his light off and then zips his sleeping bag up to his chin and drifts off to sleep…

1030 HOURS
13 DECEMBER 1987
WORLD TRADE CENTERS, NEW YORK CITY

“Slow down dude!” John Miller yells to Doyle.

“I told her we would be at the South Tower at 1030 and it’s already

1030," Doyle says running up the steps from the subway. Doyle tops the steps and goes out of site.

"No since in us running too, Aaron. We'll meet up with them when we get there," Miller tells him rolling his eyes.

"Okay," Aaron replies.

"That boy is not thinking straight," Miller says elbowing Aaron.

"He just likes her, that's all John," Aaron says to him.

"Call me Miller, I don't like the name John," he explains.

"Okay. I do not like being called by my last name, Williams. I like Aaron better," he tells him as they continue up the stairs.

As they walk outside from the subway Aaron stops dead in his tracks. "Holy shit!"

"Wow," responds Miller has they both stare up at the

World Trade Center towers.

"How can someone build something this tall?" Aaron asks.

"I don't know but, it looks like they are swaying with the clouds moving behind them," Miller tells him.

"Yeah, it's almost making me seasick," Aaron says pulling a disposable camera from his pocket. He starts taking pictures then says, "I can imagine King Kong climbing the building as I stand here."

Still gazing up at the towers, the two guys slowing continue walking when Doyle and Susan jump out from an alley and shout, "Freeze this is a hold up!"

"Very funny guys, sneaking up on us like that," Miller says to them.

"Hey!" Doyle snaps pushing Miller. "What do you mean I'm not thinking straight?"

"Someone could get hurt doing that in the city," explains Miller pushing him back.

"Y'all didn't scare me," Aaron tells Susan.

"Okay. Hey, let's have lunch on the 107th-floor food court," Susan says to them.

"That sounds cool," replies Doyle.

"I've got it," Miller says as they walk into the South Tower and up to the booth to pay. "That'll be four for the observation deck," says Miller to the lady working the booth.

"That's four tickets to the Top of the World," the lady says to him, handing him four tickets and his change.

"Thanks. Hey baby, what time do you get off work?" Miller asks the lady.

"I'm sorry ma'am," Doyle says, pushing Miller away from the window.

"What? It would have been worth her time. Did you see her rack?" Miller asks Doyle.

"Just keep walking, big mouth," replies Doyle.

"Maybe next time!" Miller shouts back to her as the elevator doors close.

"Don't be a jerk today man," Doyle tells him as the elevator starts the climb to the top.

"Oh, wow!" Aaron says as he looks out the window from the 107th floor.

"Pretty awesome isn't it?" Susan asks him.

"Yes, it is. We have to go on up to the top in a bit," he tells her.

"We will," she says, grabbing Doyle's hand and looking out the window.

"Look how clear of a day it is today Doyle," she says pulling him close to her.

"Yeah, with only a few white clouds floating in the sky. Come over and look out, Miller," Doyle yells.

"That's okay, I'm not really crazy about heights," he replies.

Susan laughs, "What? Are you afraid you might fall?"

Miller replies, "Yeah, something like that. Come on guys, I'm getting hungry."

"You hungry Susan?" Doyle asks.

"I could eat," she replies grabbing his hand.

"Hot dogs, and fries New York style," Miller says laughing.

"I'm ready to go up to the top and see where King Kong stood," Aaron says as they finish their lunch.

"You do know that he really wasn't there, right?" Miller asks him.

“Says you,” snaps Aaron.

“Okay, let’s go see King Kong,” Miller replies rolling his eyes and shaking his head.

“Come on Doyle, this is unbelievable,” Susan says tugging on his arm.

“Alright, let’s do this,” he replies, putting his military issued sock hat on.

They ride two sets of escalators up to the top of the building and walk out onto the platform that wraps around the top of the tower.

“Oh my, it’s cold up here,” Susan says snuggling up to Doyle.

Aaron walks over and looks through a pair of binoculars towards the Empire State Building, “Wow! This is so awesome!” he yells back to Doyle and Susan.

“Yes, it is!” Susan yells back as she and Doyle walk to the south side of the platform.

“If you look really hard, that small island there is the Statue of Liberty,” she says to Doyle pointing.

Miller has only walked a few feet away from the door and stands directly in the middle of the walkway, “What’s wrong, John?” Doyle yells.

“Don’t call me John, asshole!” he snaps.

“Are you going to lock up like this when we take our Airborne school?” Doyle asks him.

"Don't you worry about it!" replies Miller flipping him the bird.

"Just a few more pictures Aaron, it's too cold to stay out here long," Susan says to him.

"Yes, ma'am," he replies putting the camera back to his eye.

"I'll meet you guys back at the food court," Miller says as he disappears through the doorway.

"He's terrified of heights, isn't he?" Susan asks Doyle.

"Yes, that's the kind of guy that'll be in charge someday. You know how the guys that can't do the job always seem to be the ones they put in charge," Doyle says to her.

"I doubt he makes it out of...what do they call it, Airborne school?" Susan asks.

"Yes, that's what it's called," answers Doyle.

Aaron walks over to them, "He's mean enough to be in charge one day, I don't trust that guy."

The three head towards the escalators, "Thank you two for letting me come along today," Aaron says.

"You're welcome, Aaron," Susan tells him.

"You can hang with us anytime buddy," Doyle replies, putting his arm around him.

When they reach the food court, they see Miller sitting on a bar stool, "I'm going to the restroom before we head down," Doyle says to Susan.

"I better go too," Aaron says.

Susan sits down besides Miller as the two guys walk to the bathroom.

"I'll tell you Doyle, she's one good looking woman," Aaron says.

"Thanks, she's the best-looking woman I've ever seen," replies Doyle.

As the two guys stand at the urinals Aaron looks at him, "You think we'll ever go to war?" he asks.

"I doubt it, it seems like things are going really well around the world," Doyle responds.

"I had a dream last night that New York City was on fire. It was around 1999 to 2000 and that World War three started because of that," Aaron tells him.

"It was just a dream buddy," Doyle says as he washes his hands.

Yeah, I know, but it freaked me out," Aaron replies walking over to the sink.

"Besides, I doubt we'll ever be hit unless it comes from within," Doyle says as they walk out of the bathroom and head back over to Miller and Susan. "Ready guys?" Doyle asks.

"I need to hit the head before we go," Miller says storming off.

"What's up with him?" Aaron asks.

"Doyle, while you were in the bathroom...he hit on me," Susan tells him.

"What? I'll kick his ass," snaps Doyle.

"No, don't say anything. I don't like being around him," Susan tells him.

"You'll never see him again after today," Doyle assures her.

During the elevator ride to the ground floor, Doyle stares at Miller. Miller glances over at him every so often as if he knows Susan told him.

"Well. It sure was fun, glad I got to see you today Doyle," Susan tells him as they walk outside.

"Me too, can I have your phone number so I can call you?" Doyle asks her.

"Absolutely," she says, writing her number on the back of one of her business cards. "That's my home number and the number on the front is my work number. You can leave a message for me when I'm working and I'll call you back," says Susan as Doyle hugs her and gives her a kiss.

While they are kissing Doyle hears a low flying airplane then a large explosion coming from the South Tower. He tries to run but can't, he turns back to Susan and realizes she is no longer there. A gentleman walks past him, without saying a word he hands him a newspaper. Doyle looks down at the folded paper and notices the date. September 11, 2001...

0345 HOURS

PRESENT-DAY

TULE LAKE, SIERRA NATIONAL FOREST, CALIFORNIA

Doyle's entire body jerks as he wakes and looks around the small tent, "Aaron's dream did come true," he says outloud wiping the sweat from his forehead. He goes ahead and gets out of the sleeping bag and puts his boots on.

As he climbs out of the tent, he sees Mike sitting by a small campfire and drinking a cup of coffee. "The snow stopped about an hour ago," Mike tells him.

"How long have you been up?" Doyle asks.

"Since 0200. I found plenty of dry wood over on the other side of the lake," explains Mike.

"Anyone else in the area?" asks Doyle.

"Not that I could tell," Mike replies sipping on his coffee.

"There's a little coffee left, pour you a cup," Mike tells him.

Doyle removes a small cup out of his pack and pours the remaining coffee into it. "Have you heard any sounds?" he asks Mike.

"No, it's been very quiet," he replies looking off into the snow-covered mountains.

Doyle looks at his phone, "It's thirty-degrees, that's not too bad."

"Other than a few drifts the snow only ended up being about four-inches," Mike tells him.

"If we get some sun as well, it'll start melting," Doyle replies pulling his map out. "I think I've picked a good route for us to travel. Once we get to Edison Lake, we will go around the west end and then follow Cold Creek up to the Devil's Bathtub area."

"Unfortunately, Corey or Jonah has the high-ground, so he has the advantage," Mike says before taking another drink of coffee.

"That's not a problem Mike, he'll give away his location as we get closer so one of us can flank him."

"Once we get close to him…" Doyle starts before stopping as both of their devices on their neck starts to beep very softly.

"They're here," Mike says, standing up and pulling his 9mm out of its holster. He sits his cup of coffee down and switches clips, then looks at Doyle, "Change your clips out."

Doyle switches clips then runs over to the closest boulder and takes up a position. Mike runs over to one about twenty yards from Doyle.

Doyle sees snow fall from a tree limb to his left, "Mike, I've got movement to my left," he says.

"I saw it. Keep watching that area and I'll continue scanning the region," Mike replies.

They hear birds raising hell a few hundred yards further up the mountain as their devices stop beeping. "They were just passing through, maybe they didn't notice us. Now we have to be careful not to lead them to Jonah." Mike says as he walks over to Doyle.

Doyle stands up from off the boulder, "Let's get our tents down and

get moving." He feels his phone vibrate, "Yeah, Leon."

"Doyle, I saw where your device went off. You guys okay?"

Doyle looks over at Mike, "Yeah, we're good, it just passed by us. They're here brother."

Leon pauses a second, "I was hoping we'd get to him before they showed up. You guys be safe, I'm monitoring your movements."

"Okay, brother," Doyle says as he disconnects the phone call.

"Mike, I think that was a warning that they know we're here and that they can find us whenever they want to," he says,

"I think you're right," replies Mike as he yanks on the necklace and rips it from his neck. He walks over to a nearby tree and hangs it on a low limb, "You keep yours on, so we'll know when it's close. When we get close to Jonah, I'll stay back as you keep working towards him so you can draw the SG operator to you."

"That doesn't sound half bad," Doyle says.

After they take their tents down Mike says to him, "Once you draw the suit to you, shoot it with my bullets to deactivate it."

Doyle looks at him as Mike continues, "Then I'll kill the son-of-a-bitch."

The two guys start hiking north up the mountain, "How did you know what would deactivate it to design your bullets?" Doyle asks him.

"I can't talk about that just yet Doyle. After this mission you will

learn a lot more about those suits," Mike explains to him then stops and looks at him, "If you survive that long."

0500 HOURS
PRESENT-DAY
WAREHOUSE OUTSIDE FRESNO, CALIFORNIA

"Colonel Miller, our operator searching for Corey Prine in the Sierra National Forest just picked up two locator devices near Lake Thomas Edison," the soldier tells him.

"Welcome to California, Anderson," Miller says as he walks over to the soldier's computer screen. "Looks like we know the area Mr. Prine is in now. Alert the operator that they are close and to watch out for Anderson."

"Yes, sir," the operator replies.

"Agent Atkins, we just picked up a signal from a couple of Prine's detector devices," Miller says walking into Atkins office.

"That's wonderful news," Atkins replies looking over his fake FBI badges. "What do you think, should I be Agent West or Agent Coffee this time?" he asks Miller.

"Coffee, I think," answers Miller.

"Yeah, I was West last time, wasn't I?"

"That's correct, sir," responds Miller.

"Is our new equipment ready?" Miller asks Atkins.

"Yes, it is, you think you're ready to confront Anderson again?"

"Yes sir, I can't wait," Miller replies walking over and looking out the window.

"Okay, I'll have my men help you get ready to go. While I am in San Francisco on business you keep me posted," Atkins explains to him.

"I will sir," responds Miller. "Remember, if you call, refer to me as Agent Coffee," Atkins tells him as he opens a door to the warehouse.

They both walk through the warehouse and to a small room in the back. Atkins turns on the lights and asks, "What do you think?"

Miller stands there in awe, "It's beautiful, sir."

Atkins smiles, "It's the only one of its kind, break it and you die."

Miller nods in agreement, "Yes, sir."

Atkins turns off the lights and motions Miller to follow, "I want Prine or Jonah alive, Anderson and whoever is helping him...dead."

Atkins walks over to a Master Sergeant standing near a workbench, "Go ahead and sync it with Miller's DNA and then get him in the mountains."

"Yes, sir," the sergeant replies.

"I'll be in San Francisco for two days. The President of the United States will be there later today for a round of meetings. If you need anything do not hesitate to call," he explains to Miller and then walks away.

"Sir, if you care to follow me to the nurse on duty," the sergeant says to Miller.

"Of course, sergeant."

They walk into a small nursing station. "Okay, if you don't care to remove your shirt," the nurse says to Miller.

"Of course, ma'am," Miller responds and then takes his shirt off.

"Have you been having any problems with your port?" she asks.

"No, every so often it gets a little tender," he replies.

"Have a seat on the edge of the bed so I can look at it," she tells him.

He sits down on the bed and she walks around to look at his back. There is a small plug-in port sticking out of his skin between his shoulder blades. "The new equipment has a different prong, so I'll need to change it out before I can hook you to the computers for the download," she explains to him.

"Yes, ma'am. Whatever we need to do," he says.

She grabs a small pair of needle-nose pliers and starts working on his port and after ten-minutes she says, "Okay, I'm going to plug you in now. If you would lay on your side, please."

Miller lays down on his left side.

"Okay, here we go," she says.

"How long will it take this time?" he asks her.

"Probably two-hours or so," she replies.

She plugs a cord into his port and then types on a computer keypad. "I'll turn the tv on for you," she says as she turns it on and turns the lights out.

"Thank you," he says to her.

"Not a problem," she tells him as she leaves the room.

From a small pulpit she monitors the download and his heart rate. "Okay, you're going to feel a small vibration," she says into an intercom system. Miller's legs twitch as the download begins.

Agent Atkins walks into the pulpit, "I want you to program it as tight as you can, he's not a young pup anymore."

The nurse looks at him, "Yes, sir. But why didn't we use a younger and stronger operator?"

Atkins taps her on the shoulder, "Miller wanted to be the first to try it out."

0700 HOURS
PRESENT-DAY
THOMAS A EDISON LAKE, CALIFORNIA

"How are you doing, Mike?" Doyle asks.

"I'm good," Mike replies.

"You want to stop before we follow the creek up?" asks Doyle, stopping and looking back at him.

Mike keeps walking past him, "No, let's keep going."

They walk around Edison Lake to the mouth of Cold Creek. "I told you wrong, Cold Creek doesn't lead up to Devil's Bathtub," Doyle explains.

"Imagine that, the expert was wrong about something," replies Mike.

"We can follow it halfway up," Doyle says shaking his head.

Doyle following behind Mike says, "There's also a lot more trees from here on, we'll have to be careful not to walk into an ambush."

"That would be wise," Mike replies. They continue for another hour when the creek turns sharply to the east, "This is where we leave the creek," Doyle says.

"Okay. I need to stop and eat a bite," Mike tells him.

"That's not a problem," Doyle says, dropping his pack.

Mike sits down and pulls a sandwich out of his pack, "What do you have there, Mike?" Doyle asks.

"Peanut butter and jelly. Why, do you want a bite?" asks Mike.

"No, I've got plenty of jerky, thanks," Doyle replies.

They sit there and eat in silence before Doyle says, "Won't be much further before the trees start thinning out."

Mike stands up and says, "Then we'll be easier to see too."

"That's true," agrees Doyle as he stands up, "You ready?"

Mike does not reply but just continues up the mountain.

"I'll take that as a yes," Doyle says to him.

Before Mike can say anything both of their phones start vibrating, "Shit, that's Jonah's device going off," Mike says looking at his phone.

"He must think a suit is near him or he saw something," replies Doyle.

They both pick up their pace, "As soon as we get to the clearing, I think we should split up," Mike tells him.

"Yeah, that'll be the best way," Doyle replies.

As they reach the clearing, they hear gunshots, "Damn, I hope that's not Jonah," Doyle yells to Mike.

"I'd say it is," Mike tells him.

"Mike, you go west about fifty-yards and then continue north. I'll keep this route towards the Devil's Bathtub," explains Doyle.

"I'm on it," Mike says as he walks off to the west.

The gunshots continue as the men race to the Devil's Bathtub.

The sun shines bright on the snowcapped mountains.

Chapter Six:

TO TARSHISH

0802 HOURS
PRESENT-DAY
THE DEVIL'S BATHTUB, CALIFORNIA

Doyle moves closer to the point the gunfire is coming from and sees Jonah holding a rifle and looking into the trees.

"Show yourself, you devil!" Jonah shouts.

Doyle crawls under a pile of brush and watches Jonah pace back and forth on top of a mound.

"You will not take me to your wicked city of Nineveh!" yells Jonah.

Mike squatting down behind a large boulder on the opposite side of Jonah motions for Doyle to distract Jonah.

"What meanest thou O sleeper?" Doyle yells to Jonah.

Jonah turns and aims his rifle in Doyle's direction. "I am a Hebrew; and I fear the Lord that made the sea and dry land!" Jonah answers.

Mike starts moving closer using the noise from the windy condi-

tions in his favor as he picks up a small rock. Doyle remains still in the brush as Jonah scans the area for him.

"What shall we do unto thee, that the sea may be calm?" asks Doyle.

Jonah looks through his rifle scope then responds, "Take me up, and cast me forth into the sea."

Mike now slowly walks up behind Jonah with the rock in his right hand as Doyle watches from his position.

Doyle strains his brain trying to remember the verses from the book of Jonah.

"Lay not upon us innocent blood," he says to Jonah.

"I see you devil!" Jonah yells seeing Doyle under the brush through his scope. Just as he starts to pull the trigger Mike hits him on the head with the rock while he grabs the rifle.

"I'm the fish, bitch," Mike says to him as he falls to the ground unconscious.

Mike unloads the weapon as Doyle runs up the mound, "I thought he was going to shoot me for sure."

Mike smiles, "I think you're right for once. Help me tie him up and get him off this mound, we're sitting ducks up here."

"Has your necklace device gone off any?" Mike asks.

"No, not at all. The operator in the suit must not be close right now," Doyle answers looking around and up at the mountain peaks.

"He's not far away though," Mike says tying Jonah's feet together.

They carry Jonah off the mound and lay him at the base, then they drop both of their backpacks beside him, "Look at this," Mike tells Doyle pointing to a small opening.

Doyle walks over to get a closer look, "It's a cave someone has dug out under the mound," he says kneeling down and shining his light into.

"Looks like Jonah has been coming up here for some time digging him a place to hide," Mike tells him.

Doyle crawls through the tunnel and into the cave to inspect. "It's huge in there, Mike," Doyle says as he crawls back out.

"What are we going to do with him?" Mike asks, pointing at Jonah.

"Let's drag him in the cave, you won't believe what all he has in there."

Mike stands there staring at him, "I don't know about getting ourselves cornered in there. If the operator figures out we are in there, we won't have anywhere to escape."

Doyle looks around then asks, "How will they know we're in there? It's pretty obvious they didn't know Jonah was in there."

Mike makes a disgusted face, "Okay, I guess you're right. But I'm not crazy about it."

"Hey Mike, look at this. He's been pulling this boulder over to cover the door," Doyle says pointing at a large rock by the entrance.

"We'll need to close the entrance too, help me drag him in there," replies Mike.

They drag him to the entrance and Doyle climbs into the tunnel then Mike pushes Jonah towards him. Doyle grabs onto Jonah's shoulders and drags him the rest of the way into the cave, Mike crawls in behind Jonah and helps Doyle sit him up.

"Okay, let's prop him up over there," says Doyle.

"Here's a lantern, I'll light it so we can see better," Doyle tells him as he picks it up and lights it.

"Holy-shit. He's been planning this for some time," says Mike looking at all the gear and supplies in the cave.

"I told you that you wouldn't believe what was in here," Doyle tells him.

The ceiling is only six-feet high with wooden beams running across the width of the room. There is a row of legs in the center and on the east and west walls. Overall, the cave is ten-feet wide by twenty-feet long.

"Mike, I'm going back outside to call Leon and ask him to come get us. Then I will come back in and roll the rock in front of the entrance," Doyle says.

"He was planning on staying here a while with all these supplies," Mike tells him.

"Yeah, I'd say you're right," replies Doyle.

Doyle crawls back outside and dials Leon's number, "Hey buddy. We've got him, can you send a helicopter to come pick us up?" he asks.

"That's great Doyle. But there is no way we can fly in there with the high winds, even if you were at a lower elevation. There's a wind advisory for the rest of the day," Leon explains.

"Well...that's just great," snaps Doyle.

"Hey, while I've got you on the phone. Did you and Mike split up? I'm still showing him way down the mountain, is he?" Leon asks.

"No, he hung his device in a tree to throw the SG operator off," answers Doyle.

"Doggone it! He knows better than that. I will have to send in one of our drones to retrieve it before someone finds it. You guys lay low and wait this wind out," Leon tells him.

"Leon, we found a good shelter to wait in, but you'll have to let us know when you think they can come get us," explains Doyle.

"Okay, the best bet would be for you guys to hike down in elevation when the wind lays down tonight. At the elevation you are at I doubt the winds will ever allow us to land," Leon tells him.

"Okay, we'll hike down after the sun sets. It'll take us several hours to get back to the prior landing zone," explains Doyle.

"Yeah, that'll be the best spot. You'll have to also watch out for the SG operator looking for Jonah," Leon tells him.

"That'll be the hard part, moving down the mountain without being seen or heard," replies Doyle.

"I'll keep an eye on you guys from here. Let's set a time at 1800 hours for y'all to start down," Leon says.

"Roger-that," responds Doyle.

"Okay, brother. You guys get some rest, you are going to need it. Call me at 1800 hours so I'll know you guys are moving," explains Leon.

"Will do," Doyle says as he disconnects the phone call. He looks around and then walks over to a nearby tree to take a leak.

After he's done, he walks back to the cave entrance. "My goodness this wind is crazy," he says out loud as he places both of their backpacks into the tunnel.

Doyle crawls back into the tunnel and pulls the rock over the entrance, "Mike, he even designed a locking mechanism for the door."

Mike, sitting unloading another one of Jonah's rifles replies, "He thought of everything."

Doyle slides back into the large open room and asks, "Wonder how long it took to dig this out of the rock?"

Mike looks up at the ceiling, "I'd say years. He had to blast most of it out I am sure. There are also a few tunnels behind those posters leading to two smaller rooms, not much in those rooms though. I've unloaded every weapon that I've found," Mike tells him.

"Okay, thanks Mike," Doyle replies.

"What's the game plan?" Mike asks.

"The wind is too bad for them to come get us even if we hiked down in elevation. Plus, with an SG operator in the area it will probably be good for us to hole-up here until it gets dark," Doyle explains as he removes his boots. "These new boots are killing me," he says.

"Now we wait for sleeping-beautiful to wake," Mike says leaning back against the rock wall.

"That's right. Mike you go ahead and get some rest, I'll watch him," Doyle tells him.

"Okay. What time are we pulling out?" Mike asks.

"1800 hours. That means we have eight hours here," replies Doyle.

Mike thinks a second then says, "I'll rest the first three hours then you can have the next three."

Doyle gives him the thumbs up, "Sounds good."

"That way we'll have a few hours to get him ready and eat something," Mike says.

"You know, I was thinking that the SG suits are probably equipped with night-vision," says Doyle.

"They are. But they also know we have our device to detect them and that he has his tool to disable them," Mike explains.

"They'll try and ambush us then. Hopefully, Jonah will cooperate with us on the way down," Doyle tells him.

"I'll explain that it's up to him if we deliver him dead or alive," replies Mike.

Doyle laughs, "I'm sure he'll take that good."

"We're at an elevation of almost ten-thousand feet, the drop zone is at an elevation of six-thousand seven-hundred feet. Hiking in the dark and with a hostage might take a while," Doyle tells Mike.

"That it will," replies Mike.

Doyle pulls his map out of his pocket, "Mike, go ahead and try to get some sleep."

Mike pulls his sleeping bag from his pack and crawls back into one of the other rooms.

1300 HOURS
PRESENT-DAY
INSIDE JONAH'S CAVE

Mike crawls back into the main room, "Jonah hasn't woken up yet?" he asks.

"Not yet, but he's been making noises. I don't think it'll be long now, you smacked him good," Doyle says to him.

"I'll tell you one thing, that small room is cold," Mike tells him, rolling up his sleeping bag.

"It must be closer to the outside than this one. The wind is still howling out there," Doyle says.

"Are you going to try and sleep?" Mike asks him.

"I doubt it, I'm not sleepy, I'll just lay here until he wakes up," Doyle replies.

Mike slides over close to Jonah and kicks him, "Wake up. I know you can hear me, Corey."

He opens his eyes and looks at Mike, "My name is Jonah."

Mike grabs him by his shoulders and sets him up, "I've never called you Jonah...your name is Corey."

Jonah looks at him, "How'd you find me?"

"You two know each other?" Doyle asks.

"Yeah, we've worked together for years at Edwards Air Force Base," replies Mike.

"I'm no longer that sinner, I'm now Jonah the preacher."

Doyle sits up, "What do you mean by working together, on what?" he asks.

"Go ahead, Corey, tell him," Mike says.

"My name is Jonah you devil," he says to Mike.

"Okay, I'm not going to fight about it no more...Jonah," Mike tells him.

"Why am I tied like an animal?" Jonah asks.

"I didn't trust you to behave while I rested," says Mike.

"Hello, what did you guys work on?" Doyle asks again.

"We worked on the invisible suit technology and other projects at Edwards," Mike tells him.

"You mean I was forced to work on those abominations," Jonah replies.

"Well, you never complained about the money you were paid. What was it...two-million?" asks Mike.

"Can you please untie me?" he asks, holding up his hands.

Doyle nods to Mike to go ahead and untie him, "You going to be a good boy?" Mike asks Jonah.

"Yes, I will," he replies.

Mike grabs Jonah's arm, "Keep in mind that we are both armed and won't think twice about shooting you." Mike cuts the ropes from his hands and legs, "I'm serious, no funny stuff."

Jonah rubs his wrist as he looks at Doyle, "So, you're the famous Anderson that Aaron has talked about for years."

Doyle leans back against the wall, "That's me, so you know Aaron too, uh? Hey Mike, will you fill him in on our game plan?" Doyle asks as he puts his hat over his face.

Jonah stands up, "Hang on before you start. There's no since we're sitting here with just that lantern, this whole place is battery-powered," he explains as he flips a couple of switches. Small led lights come on around the ceiling and four computer screens light up.

"There's a battery room behind that cabinet," Jonah says pointing

to the other side of the room. He walks over and swings the cabinet away from the wall, "Come on, Mike."

"Doyle, you try and rest. I'm going back there with him," Mike tells him.

"Roger-that," Doyle replies.

Jonah and Mike crawl down another tunnel that leads to a room as large as the main room. "This room has a separate ventilation system in case I have issues with the batteries. There's also an emergency exit in here too if I need to escape fast," Jonah explains.

"How long did it take you to build this?" asks Mike.

"It took just shy of five years, three years to dig and blast it out then the last two to complete the inside," Jonah tells him.

"What are the other two small rooms for?" Mike asks. "Those are going to be bedrooms once I haul the special built beds up. The parts are still at Edwards," Jonah explains.

"Those rooms are colder than the main room," he tells Jonah.

"They shouldn't be now since I restored the power, they have heating coils under the floor. I ran them under the floor to keep from melting any snow on top outside," replies Jonah.

"Those two bedrooms are the only floors that I poured concrete in to cover the heating coils," Jonah explains. "The main room and this room have enough equipment in them to keep the rooms warm," he continues.

"You did a good job on this, but why build it?" Mike asks him.

"For when everything falls apart and the Antichrist is on the earth," Jonah tells him.

"So, you believe all that folklore uh?" Mike asks.

He looks at Mike and says, "I pray ye that your flight will not be in the winter."

"I don't know what that means," Mike tells him.

"For in those days shall be affliction, such as was not from the beginning of the creation which GOD created unto this time, neither shall be," replies Jonah in a stern voice.

"What affliction?" Mike asks.

"Take ye heed, watch and pray for ye know not when the time is," Jonah says, looking directly at him.

"Okay, we're done here," says Mike as he crawls back through the tunnel to the main room.

"Now learn a parable of the fig tree!" Jonah yells to him.

"What's he yelling about?" Doyle asks with the hat still over his eyes.

"He was acting normal then all of a sudden he switched back to nutsville," answers Mike sitting down by the computer monitors.

"What'd you say to upset him?" asks Doyle.

"Nothing," he replies watching Jonah crawling out of the tunnel.

Jonah closes the cabinet then says to Mike, "Those monitors show you everything outside around this bunker. It's an animation of what's going on out there, normal cameras can give away your location."

"You calm now? No more crazy man fits I hope…Jonah."

He just looks at Mike, "How you like the animation?"

"I thought it looked like the project you were working on at Edwards," Mike says.

"It is. Plus, my owl drone is in a tree nearby," replies Jonah.

"What's an owl drone?" Doyle asks.

Jonah smiles then says, "It's a normal drone that looks so much like a real owl, that other owls even think it's real. If I need to get a closer look of something, I fly it over to check it out. It flies like a real owl too."

Doyle raises his hat up then asks, "It flaps its wings?"

Jonah nods his head, "It does indeed, Doyle."

"That's freaking crazy. Hey, why are you up here hiding?" Doyle asks him.

"I didn't want to do the kind of work they want me to anymore," Jonah says pointing at Mike.

"You signed a contract and accepted payment," Mike replies.

"I don't care...I'm done," Jonah tells him.

"That's not how it works, and you know that," says Mike.

"It does for me!" snaps Jonah.

Mike places his hand on his gun holster, "You going to get crazy again? I will shoot your ass right here. Listen, this is going to go down one of two ways. One, you follow us down the mountain and back to Edwards. Two, we carry a body bag with you in it and back to Edwards," Mike explains to him.

"I thought we were on a rescue mission and to save him from the SG?" Doyle asks.

"We are but it's also a mission to retrieve the Patriots property," Mike replies.

"No one owns me but GOD," Jonah shouts.

"Just relax and stop yelling," Mike says patting his gun holster again. "Who funded this technology you're using in this cave?" Mike asks Jonah.

He does not reply but just stares at Mike.

"That's what I thought, you didn't have the billions of dollars it took to make this equipment. Nor did you have access to the alien crafts to reverse their technology. So, you are their property," Mike tells him.

"Wait a second. Alien craft? What?" Doyle asks.

"That's right. But we will talk about that when we get to Edwards. Right now, we must figure out how to get back down the mountain alive," Mike replies and then continues. "There is an SG operator waiting out there to kill you Jonah, then me and Doyle. So, it's time you get your head on straight and help us get out of here and to the

helicopter tonight."

Before anyone could say anything one of the computer monitors starts flashing. "Looks like we have company," Jonah says sliding over to the computer.

"My necklace is not beeping," Doyle says.

"It won't, too much rock to pick up the signal in here," Jonah explains to him.

"He's looking for us, see him standing there by that tree?" Jonah asks Mike.

"That little squiggly line?" asks Mike.

"Yep, that's him. Oh, there he goes flying now," says Jonah.

"We're going to have to deal with him now before we try to make it to the helicopter," Doyle tells them.

"I agree, he needs to be removed," Mike says.

"That's what I was working on when you hit me on the head," replies Jonah.

"But how do we go about it now is the real question," Doyle says sliding over beside them.

"We're going to have to go out there and confront him, guys," says Mike.

"If I can get him to within fifty yards of me, I can disable his suit with this," Jonah replies, holding up a small remote looking thing.

"How long will it knock it out?" Doyle asks.

"For maybe fifteen-minutes. It normally takes about that long to reboot the suit where the jet pack will work. But the invisibility takes closer to thirty-minutes," explains Jonah.

"That means we have fifteen minutes to kill the operator then," Mike tells them.

"That is correct however, we can also cut the wire to the plug that connects the operator to the suit. If it does not detect a heartbeat for three minutes it will self-destruct," Jonah replies.

"Why three-minutes?" asks Doyle. "Because it takes five minutes to successfully shut the program down. That way if the operator is killed-in-action, the enemy does not have time to remove the suit and steal it, replies Jonah.

He continues, "There are two separate programs running that suit, my device just shuts down the program that controls the operation of the suit. The other program links with the operator's nervous system. If it is interrupted for three minutes, either by the operator being killed or the main cord being removed or cut, it self-destructs."

"That sounds bad if you have some kind of problem with it," Doyle says.

"These suits are so top-secret and so dangerous that they'll sacrifice the operator to keep them out of the wrong hands," Mike explains.

"Well, they did end up in the wrong hands, remember? That is why we are sitting here trying to figure out how to kill one," snaps Jonah.

"True. But they were not stolen off an operator's back. They were

stolen from one of our warehouses long before we were in the game," Mike tells him.

"Doyle, there's even an operator in a control room that can put the suit in self-destruct mode as well...at least on these older models," Jonah explains.

"What do you mean? They all have that option, even the new ones, right?" Mike asks.

Jonah looks around the room, then replies, "Oh yeah, that's right."

Doyle nods his head as he sits there listening to both, then he asks pointing at the monitor, "What do we do about this guy that is searching for us?"

Jonah lets out a laugh, "He'll never find us in here. Just like Doyle's device will not pick him up in here, his device will not pick us up either."

Mike looks at him, "But he will see us as soon as we open that door."

Jonah jumps to his feet, "That's it, Mike!"

"What's it?" Mike asks.

"We wait until he gets close to the door and then we open it and I hit him with my deactivation device shutting down the suit. One of you guys will exit through the emergency door at the same time and ambush the operator from behind while he's focused on me," Jonah explains.

"That just might work," Doyle tells him.

"Doyle, you exit out the emergency door and I'll help Jonah open this door. Make sure you have the correct clip in your weapon," Mike explains to him.

"Now we need to figure out how to get the operator close enough to the door for this to work," says Doyle.

"I hate to do this to my little buddy. But I could use my owl to draw the operator close. Have the owl fly close to him then land by the door," explains Jonah.

"How exactly will you get the operators attention?" Mike asks him.

"The owl has a speaker built into it. If the operator does not come over, I can say things through that speaker to draw him close," responds Jonah.

"Well, that's the plan then. It's only 1500 hours so, that means we have three-hours to take care of this guy to still make it to the pickup zone in time," Doyle tells them.

"It will take about twenty-minutes to power up the owl and hopefully the doors to his nests are not blocked or frozen," Jonah explains.

"Yeah, let's hope not," Mike says.

Jonah types on one of the computer keyboards, "Okay, he is booting up. Doyle, come back to the battery room so I can show you how to open that door."

The owl's eyes light up inside his nest.

The SG operator flies to the top of Graveyard Peak and searches the area for Jonah.

Chapter Seven:

BELLY OF THE FISH

1530 HOURS
PRESENT-DAY
THE DEVIL'S BATHTUB, CALIFORNIA

"Okay, guys the owl is online. Let us hope the door opens," Jonah tells them as he watches on one of the monitors. The screen shows the inside of the owl's nest through cameras in its eyes, "Alright, they opened. We should be good to go once the SG operator comes back around. As soon as I see him, I will put my helmet on so I can control the owl," explains Jonah pointing to a helmet hanging on the wall.

"What, is that like virtual reality or something?" Doyle asks him.

"It's like a thousand times better than that. Once I put the helmet on it is like I am the owl, there are two rings I slip over my fingers on my right hand to control the flight. I start with a closed fist then open it to take flight. I move my hand to control its flight along with the movement of my head," Jonah tells him.

Jonah continues, "My eyes control the cameras in its eyes, If I blink fast it takes pictures, if I squint it will zoom in. There is a button between the rings I can press, and it will just fly around and record the area. If I hold the button it will automatically return to its nest and close the doors. After five minutes in the nest, it will power down. I can also program a mission for it to do on its own at a set time, it can go up to one-hundred miles round trip before it needs charging."

"That's unbelievable," says Doyle.

"You haven't seen anything yet," replies Jonah.

Doyle slides over to his boots and puts them on then looks at Mike, "You ready to take this guy out?"

Sitting there with his eyes closed meditating, Mike replies, "The question is, are you ready?"

Doyle stands up and stretches his legs, "I was trained for this kind of moment. It's all instinct now, I've done it several hundred times."

"True, but never against an invisible suit," replies Mike.

"As far I know," Doyle says laughing.

Mike puts his jacket on then checks to make sure his extra clips are still inside. "Doyle, you'll need to go with live rounds since Jonah is taking the suit down with his device," Mike explains to him.

"Roger-that," he replies.

Jonah watches the monitors for any movement as Mike and Doyle get their gear together.

"Mike, go ahead and unlatch that door. It does make a little noise that the SG operator could hear," Jonah tells him.

Mike crawls over and unlatches it, "It's ready."

Doyle reaches in his backpack and pulls out two wireless earphones with a microphone attached, "Mike, let's use these headsets to communicate since the wind is still gusting."

Mike takes one from him and places it in his ear, "Testing 1, 2, 3."

Doyle gives him the thumbs up then asks in his mic, "You copy?"

Mike replies, "Ten-four."

Jonah hands Mike his remote device, "Mike, since I'll be flying the owl you use this. When I say, you open that door and press the button as fast as you can. You'll know if it works because you'll hear the suit start making loud noises."

Mike grabs the remote and looks it over then answers, "Okay, I've got it."

Jonah looks at Doyle, "Keep in mind that this operator could be and probably is armed. The device doesn't disable any of his weapons, just the suit."

"I understand, Jonah," Doyle replies sitting down beside him.

"I bet you've seen a lot of action in your career," Jonah says to him.

"You could say that, more than I can count," Doyle says, pulling his hat back down over his eyes.

Mike closes his eyes again to meditate as Jonah reaches up and flips

the lights off. “You guys rest, I’ll keep watching the screens for him,” Jonah tells them.

Jonah takes his journal off the desk and starts writing in it:

-1558 hours.

-Bunker with Anderson and Rosen.

-Waiting on SG operator to show himself.

-Going to try and eliminate the operator.

1600 HOURS
PRESENT-DAY
HERBST THEATRE, SAN FRANCISCO

“This is a new day for San Francisco. For the first time in a long time, it is Republican ran, and the homeless rate is the lowest of all the major cities in the United States. Thank you, San Francisco,” the President of the United States says as he exits the stage.

“Agent Coffee, glad you could join us today,” the FBI Director tells him.

“Thank you, sir,” Coffee replies walking out of the theatre’s main auditorium.

The FBI director follows him into the hallway then asks, “Are you going to join us at Alcatraz Island for the ceremony later?”

Agent Coffee replies, “Yes sir, I’ll be there.”

The director turns and walks down another hallway and out of

sight.

Coffee continues towards the exit when he hears someone behind him, “Agent, hold up a second.”

“Senator Douglas, I didn’t see you standing there,” Coffee tells him.

They walk outside, “I wanted to tell you that I stopped by the warehouse in Fresno before I came here,” the Senator tells him.

“You did? What for?” Coffee asks sounding caught off guard.

“I was going to talk to Miller, but he was on a table hooked to a computer,” the Senator replies as they cross the street to City Hall.

“Why are you fitting Miller for that suit?” the Senator asks.

“He volunteered for it,” Coffee replies.

“You do understand that once the download is complete, he’ll have to remain up to date on the software or he’ll die. You do know, that right?” asks the Senator.

“I explained that to him but, he still wanted to move forward,” replies Coffee.

The Senator stops, “Listen Atkins…I’m not calling you Coffee. Miller is out, fired. The director is not happy how things turned out with the Wolfgang boy. I told the other guys there to make sure Miller is out of the building as soon as he comes off the table.”

“But Miller will die,” Atkins says as he starts walking then asks, “What about me?”

The Senator puts his arm around him as they walk, “In the morn-

ing, you're flying to DC to meet with the director."

"Why does he want to see me?" Atkins asks.

The Senator laughs, "Well, let us just say you've made some really questionable decisions lately. And he doesn't even know about you fitting Miller for that new suit." After the Senator tells him that he stops, raises his hand, a Limo pulls up and he climbs in. The back-window lowers, "Stay in touch now, you hear?" the Senator tells him.

Atkins stands there and watches the limo drive away, "I really hate that old man," he says out loud.

Atkins continues walking for several blocks then walks into the Whitmer Hotel. He walks through the lobby, enters an elevator, and presses his room floor. He feels his phone vibrate, "This is Coffee."

There is a moment of silence… "Where are you Agent Atkins?" Miller asks.

"I'm back at the hotel. Where are you?" Atkins asks just before the call disconnects. He exits the elevator and walks down the hallway to his room door looking around to see if anyone is around.

He walks into his room and throws his jacket on the bed, picks up a cup and fills it with water. "What in the hell is going on," he says out loud walking to the window.

"You tell me," he hears someone whisper.

He turns around and sees nobody, he cups his hand and pours a little water into it. He tosses the water towards the center of the room.

The water flies through the air and spreads out, some of it hits the wall while the rest of it stops in midair and falls to the floor.

Before Atkins can say anything, he is slammed into the window and slowly picked up off the ground, "Your time has come and gone, Atkins," Miller says. "You think you guys can fire me just like that?" asks Miller.

"I didn't have anything to do with it," Atkins says, trying to fight himself loose.

"You think I believe that!" yells Miller.

"How did you get out of the warehouse with that suit?" Atkins asks.

"I killed everyone that stood in my way. Now, I have the latest model plus the self-destruct remote," Miller tells him.

A small dent appears behind Atkins' left ear, "Wait, Miller let's talk about this." Blood starts to run down the side of his neck.

"Time to talk is long gone," Miller says as he pushes a knife into Atkins head, killing him instantly.

He lays Atkins on the floor then walks out onto the balcony and fires up the jetpack and flies away. Several people on the ground watching the Presidential motorcade driving past sees the vapor from the jetpack, "What the heck was that?" one of them asks.

Several secret service agents look up toward the hotel, they radio the nearby snipers, "You guys see anything near the Whitmer Hotel?"

A sonic boom rattles downtown San Francisco as the motorcade

speeds up and law enforcement agent's scatter.

Senator Douglas stops just before he enters his hotel and says to his detail, "Tell me that was not what it sounded like. Call Fresno just to make sure everything is okay."

One of the men in his security detail pulls his phone out, "I'm on it, sir."

The Senator stands there looking up at the sky.

1645 HOURS
PRESENT-DAY
INSIDE JONAH'S BUNKER

"Guys, he's back," Jonah says to them.

"I was afraid you were going to say that" Doyle replies, getting up.

"I'm deploying the owl," says Jonah.

"Okay. Why couldn't they have used one of our suits to fight this guy?" asks Doyle.

"They're not available," replies Jonah.

"Where have I heard that before?" Doyle asks.

"Two of them are in Afghanistan and the newer model is always with the President," explains Mike.

"Got it. I'm heading back to the emergency door, give me the word when you're ready," Doyle tells them as he heads to the tunnel.

Mike slides over to the door and watches the computer monitor. He sees through the owl's eyes as it flies overhead.

"I see the operator," Jonah says with the helmet on. "I'm going to fly the owl near him," he tells Mike.

"Roger-that," Mike replies.

Jonah flies the owl within twenty yards of the operator, circles it over his head, and then lands it on a boulder near the entrance to the cave. "He's moving towards it, Mike," Jonah tells him.

"That's great. Get ready Doyle," Mike says into his mic.

"Come on buddy, keep walking," Jonah says, watching the operator on one of the screens inside the helmet.

"Okay Mike, do it!" he shouts.

Mike rolls the door open and sticks his arm outside while pressing the button on the remote.

"He's seen you, but...it took, the suit is shutting down," Jonah says.

They can hear loud popping sounds coming from outside, "Now, Doyle," Mike tells him into his mic.

Doyle slams the gear shift backwards and the emergency door pops open, he crawls out and runs up on top of the mound. He pulls his 9mm out of its holster and moves closer to the operator's position, who is pushing buttons on a keypad attached to his forearm.

Doyle drops to one knee and fires a shot hitting the operator in the chest. The operator steps back and in one motion throws a grenade

towards Doyle. The grenade hits the ground ten feet from Doyle, he jumps off the mound just as the explosion goes off causing him to flip.

"You son-of-a-bitch!" Mike yells as he runs out of the cave firing his pistol at the operator.

The operator runs off to the north and up the mountain.

"Doyle, you okay?" Mike asks.

"No, my knee...I think I blew my knee out," Doyle replies holding onto his knee.

Jonah runs over to him and inspects his leg, "You might have fractured your tibia too," he tells him looking at his leg.

"You take care of him; I'm going after this guy. We can't let him get away," Mike explains as he starts walking north.

"He's bleeding quite a bit," Mike says to himself leaning down and inspecting the ground. "Doyle, give your headset to Jonah," he says to Doyle through his mic.

"Here you go, he wants to talk to you," Doyle explains, handing Jonah his headset.

"Go ahead, Mike. This is Jonah."

Mike stops to reply, "You said it takes fifteen minutes to reboot the suit so the jetpack can work, correct?" he asks.

"That is correct, Mike." Jonah answers.

"Okay, he's bleeding really bad so I'm sure I'll find him before that,"

replies Mike as he starts moving at a steady pace while the wind blows snow up in his face.

“There’s no reason to put this off!” he shouts. “I know you’re wounded!”

He continues to follow the tracks in the snow that is now over six inches deep. The landscape is mostly barren at this elevation with several deep drifts. The drops of blood beside the tracks are now darker in color. He holds his left hand in front of his face to block the windblown snow as he slowly moves forward.

“Mike, have you found him yet?” Jonah asks over the headset.

“Not yet, but I’m close,” he replies.

There’s slight movement off to his left, “There you are,” he says looking at the operator sitting with his back to a large boulder. Mike, keeping his weapon aimed at the operator as he approaches him with caution.

“You move an inch and I’ll shoot you dead,” he tells the motionless operator.

“They’re coming for you, Mike. You’ll never make it off this mountain alive,” the operator tells him.

“You’re a woman?” Mike asks.

She holds her hands up showing Mike she is not reaching for a weapon and removes the helmet, “You don’t think a woman can do this job?” she asks lying the helmet on the ground beside her.

"Is that you, Amy?" asks Mike sounding shocked.

"Of course, it is. Who were you expecting?" she says as she coughs up a small amount of blood.

"Anyone but you…But why…he's your brother and you came here to kill him?" Mike asks, walking closer.

"I wasn't going to kill him; I was going to transport him back to Fresno so he could complete the work on our new suit. I came here to kill you and Anderson," she explains to him.

"What new suit?" asks Mike.

"He didn't tell you that he had designed a new suit for us?" Amy asks coughing up blood again.

"No, he didn't."

"Well, you're about to see it, or at least hear it soon. He is on his way here, I just radioed and told him I was hit. He will kill you and Anderson, then he will take Jonah with him. You can't get out of here Mike," she tells him.

"Him who?" Mike asks.

Amy again coughs up blood then says, "Miller…You're going to die on this mountain, Mike."

"Come on, Doyle. Let's get you back in the cave," says Jonah.

"Don't move me yet, I need a splint on it first. I have one in my backpack," replies Doyle.

"Okay, I'll be right back," Jonah says, running to the cave.

"In my pack there's also a bottle of pain killers, bring that too!" Doyle yells.

The owl, sitting on the boulder nearby, turns its head and looks at Doyle.

"What are you looking at?" asks Doyle as it suddenly flies away and back into its nest. Doyle watches as the doors close and the owl disappears from his sight.

Jonah returns a short time later with the gear needed, "Here's your pain meds, now let's get this knee immobilizer on you."

"I need it tight but not too tight, I still have to walk off this mountain tonight," Doyle tells him.

"Okay, but first, we have to get you back in the cave. Just in case there is another operator up here," Jonah says.

"Let's hope not, plus, that's their only functioning suit right now," replies Doyle.

"Yeah...about that, I meant to tell you guys earlier that they have a new suit," Jonah tells him.

Doyle reaches up and grabs Jonah by the throat, "What do you mean?" he asks, pulling him closer to his face.

"I'm sorry, I was going to tell you," Jonah answers as Doyle pushes him away…

"How long have you been working with the suits?" Mike asks Amy.

"For years...tell me Mike, why did you flip?" she asks.

"It's like this, Amy. Once I found out the weapons that we were moving were being used against American troops I could not be a part of that. The Ambassador and I felt the same way about it. Then when our guys were attacked in Benghazi and some were killed including the Ambassador, I told myself that even if it took the rest of my life, I was going kill those responsible," replies Mike stepping one step closer.

"We knew that you were getting weak, you were supposed to be killed there too, you know. Your boss was going to squeal about the US arming ISIS. We couldn't allow that, so all of you had to die," she explains to him with blood running out of her nose.

"Well, I guess God had different plans for me. Now, I will give you a few seconds to get right with your maker, then you will go to meet him," Mike tells her.

Mike takes a few steps backwards, "Say your peace," he tells her looking down at the ground.

"You know what Mike, screw you! Miller will be here soon; we'll see who's talking then!" she yells spitting blood out of her mouth.

He sees her pushing buttons on the keypad then hears the jetpack making noises, "Father, have mercy on her soul," he prays.

He walks up to her, "You chose unwisely." He aims his 9mm at her as she screams and then shoots her between the eyes. "Wish it could

have worked out differently," he says to her as she slumps over dead.

"Come in Jonah," Mike says into the radio.

"Go ahead Mike, this is Jonah."

"The operator has been killed. The suit should self-destruct soon," Mike tells him.

"Okay, sounds good. Who was the operator, Mike?" he asks.

"I didn't know the guy," Mike says.

"Mike, I'm taking Doyle back into the cave. You should hurry back too so we can lock the door," explains Jonah.

"Roger-that. On my way," he replies as a loud explosion from the suit erupts behind him. He stops and looks back, "Damn, that was something," he says out loud pulling his phone out.

He phones Leon, "Leon, we may have a problem. I just eliminated the operator up here and it was Amy Leek."

Leon pauses, "For real?" he asks.

"Yes, for real. She also said before I shot her, that Miller is on his way in a new suit," explains Mike.

"New suit? That is strange," says Leon.

"Is it? How come I get the feeling that you guys knew they had a new suit?" he asks him.

"Mike, I would have told you guys if had known," Leon tells him.

"I hope that's true Leon," he replies.

"Where are you guys at, still in the cave?" asks Leon.

"I'm heading back there now, there's something else too, Doyle is injured. She threw a grenade at him causing him to fall and he broke his leg or blew out his knee," Mike tells him.

"Holy-cow! The bulletproof Anderson has finally been injured," exclaims Leon.

"Well, if it's true that Miller is on his way, I'm down a man," Mike says.

"Brother, there's nothing I can do for you right now. No one else is available, you'll have to fight him with whatever help Jonah can give you," says Leon.

"I'm not sure an eighty-year-old is going to be very much help," Mike says.

"I understand your concern Mike. But these are the cards we have been dealt. I could send two drones up to cover you guys, but if Miller sees them, he can take them out with that suit. Plus, they are not equipped to see those suits...So they would be very little help. The wind still hasn't let up any, you guys stay put in the cave until 1900 hours then start down," explains Leon.

"Sounds good, I'll be in touch at 1900 hours," replies Mike...

"Oh good, give me a hand Mike," Jonah says as he sees Mike walking towards them.

"I'm only two-hundred and fifteen pounds!" Doyle snaps.

Mike runs over and helps Jonah get him to the entrance, "I've got it now," Doyle tells them.

"I'm going around to the back side and close that emergency door," Jonah tells Mike.

Mike nods his head as he watches Doyle crawl into the cave, "Just hurry up!" he yells to Jonah.

Doyle slides over near the computer monitors and lays down, "Shit, this hurts like hell," he says as he props his leg up on his backpack.

Mike waits outside as Jonah returns, "Get in, we've got something to talk about!" Mike yells over the howling wind.

After they both are back in the cave Jonah says to Mike, "Hang on one minute, I've got to go lock that emergency door."

Mike nods in agreement then turns to Doyle, "You need anything?" He asks.

"A new leg would be nice," Doyle replies then asks, "What time is it?"

"It is 1750 hours. I talked with Leon and we've pushed our exit time back to 1900 hours," Mike explains.

"Okay, that'll give the medicine time to kick in, hopefully," replies Doyle.

"We've got another issue too, Doyle," Mike says.

"Yeah, what's that?"

"It's Miller. He's heading this way according to that operator," Mike replies.

"Really...that's interesting," Doyle tells him sitting up.

"No don't get up, Doyle you rest that leg," says Mike motioning for Doyle to lay back down.

Jonah returns from the battery room, "What did you want to talk about, Mike?" he asks.

"When were you going to tell us about the new suit you designed for the Shadow Government?" Mike asks him.

"Now Mike, I meant to, but the subject never came up," Jonah replies.

"What do you mean the subject didn't come up? Don't you think that is something we should know about?" Yells Mike.

"I know, I know...sorry," Jonah says.

"Sorry...really?" asks Mike.

"Mike, he told me while you were chasing the SG operator down," Doyle tells him.

"That's nice. We could have walked into a trap going out there not knowing there's another suit, a new and improved one at that!" snaps Mike.

"I know Mike, it's my fault, I should have told you," replies Jonah.

Mike draws his weapon and points it at Jonah, "What else have you forgotten to tell us?" he asks.

Jonah raises his hands up, "The remote doesn't work on this new suit," he says closing his eyes tight.

"Well, isn't that just great! According to the SG operator, your buddy Miller is in it and headed here. So, tell me preacher-man, how do we deal with this new suit?" Mike asks him.

"I'm working on it, Mike. There is a way but it's not going to be easy and only I can do it," Jonah tells him.

"I'm all ears," Mike says lowering his weapon.

"I'll have to get really close to him, then with this device," Jonah says holding up another small remote. "It should disrupt the controls of the suit," he says.

"How do you plan to get that close to him?" Mike asks.

"I'm not sure just yet, Mike," Jonah says.

"Well, you better figure it out. We have just over an hour then we are heading for the helicopter," Mike tells him.

"I'll think of something...I promise," whispers Jonah.

"No promises just do it!" snaps Mike.

The sun has now set with darkness covering the mountain.

Trees sway in the high winds.

Chapter Eight:

MAN WITH A GREEN FACE

18 10 HOURS
PRESENT-DAY
INSIDE JONAH'S BUNKER

Jonah sits down in front of the computer, "Mike, I believe I can program this remote to disable the control functions on the new suit. The only problem is that I can't use it remotely, I'll have to plug it into a port on the back of the suit itself."

"And how do you plan on doing that?" Mike asks as he stands up. "You just keep working on it, Jonah. I'm going to one of the back rooms to lay down, my head is killing me," he tells him.

After Mike exits the room, Doyle asks Jonah, "I hear you were a Frogman?"

"Yes sir, I was back in another lifetime."

"How long did you serve?" asks Doyle.

"1958 thru 1970, I served in Vietnam. I was an advisor for the

training of the Army of the Republic of Vietnam commandos." Jonah turns around away from the computer monitor, then continues. "I was deployed to South Vietnam in 1962, we spent a year training before we began covert missions in 1963. We worked for the Central Intelligence Agency."

"How many missions were you a part of?" asks Doyle.

Jonah looks at him, "Just in Vietnam?"

"Yes," Doyle replies.

"I don't know, thirty or forty covert missions, I've lost count over the years. But we did operations daily to support the overall mission. I spent most of my time in the water blowing things up and setting traps for the Viet Cong. We were free to do what we had to do to successfully meet our objective. The rest of the war was all political, men weren't put in positions to succeed."

"Unfortunately, the wars I served in were political," Doyle says.

"What are you talking about Doyle? They all are and have been since the dawn of time. Politics and religion are the same thing. The Seals at one time were run differently; they were not controlled by politics. But I guess that's not the case today."

"You were one of the men with green faces," replies Doyle.

"That I was. We put fear in the enemy's hearts. They claimed if you saw one of us you did not live to talk about it. That was not the case, there were many I let walk away," Jonah says.

"You had to feel a lot of pride working for the unit that President

John F. Kennedy helped organize," Doyle tells him.

"Oh, we did...until the organization we worked for killed him. Although, after my enlistment was up, I went to work for the CIA in 1970 working on these suits."

"You've been working on those things all this time?" asks Doyle.

"I have. That reminds me, Doyle. I have got one of the models from the 70's right here," Jonah tells him walking over to a chest and unlocking it. He opens the lid and pulls out a one-piece jumpsuit that has wires and hoses running to a small box attached to a backpack.

"You have to wear this backpack on the outside of the suit, these models didn't have the jetpack back then. This backpack has the invisibility device inside, it makes a lot of noises that sound like steam venting off."

"Holy-shit!" exclaims Doyle.

"Cool uh? They are not completely invisible but, with some cover like jungle or darkness, they work well. And, with these you do not have to be plugged into the computer system running it. Because there is no computer. I invented face paint for this model that also works very well, it is a green-camo paint that blends with the suit. If you are standing still your face is almost invisible. As you know, the newer suits use a helmet."

"Did you choose green because of Vietnam?" Doyle asks him.

"I did indeed. I lost so many friends over there, I thought it would be a good way to honor them. Plus, the green camo worked the best

for both invisible and non-invisible situations. Black was the best color for the invisibility but not for when the suit was in motion. There's a lot more that goes into the colors themself but that's all classified."

Jonah lays the suit on top of a table then places the backpack beside it. The two guys just look at the suit for a few minutes until Doyle says, "Why don't you use that suit to get close to Miller."

"I don't know if it still works well enough. Plus, my long beard will get in the way or he will see it," Jonah replies as he rubs his beard.

"How else can you get close enough to him. I think it is the best way to place that remote on him. I think it will work Jonah."

"Well...I guess it might work. Miller has never been around this model in operation, so he will not have any clue what the sounds are coming out of it. We will have to get him close to my location, I do not move as well as I once did. I'm eighty-years-old now."

"We can shoot his suit with one of Mike's bullets so you can see him. You think that might work?" asks Doyle.

"Those rounds won't shut his suit down. I designed those suits to be resistant to those. However, it will disrupt the invisibility for a few seconds as the program works to stay running. You won't see him completely but just enough to know where he's at maybe," explains Jonah.

"That's all we need. Now, we must figure out a way to draw him in so you can get close enough to place that remote on him," Doyle tells him.

Jonah sits back down by the computer then says, "I know the perfect bait."

"Yeah...what's that?" Doyle asks.

Jonah looks at Doyle and smiles, "You. He hates you with a passion and wants you dead. You can draw him to you because he will not just shoot you, he wants you to suffer and for you to know he's the reason for your suffering."

"I've never understood why he hated me so bad. That hatred started early on for some reason, I mean way back in AIT training," responds Doyle.

"He was jealous that you landed Susan, he has a thing for her, even to this day. He told me once several years ago that you stole his soulmate right out of his hands," Jonah explains to him.

"They never even dated, that's crazy talk. She did not like him from the get-go. She thought he was a jerk and told me that she didn't like him around, so I kept him away from her," Doyle says.

"I don't know, I'm just telling you what I think it is," replies Jonah.

"Anyway…So, you think the suit thing will work?" Doyle asks changing the subject.

"I think it might. Let me scan the area for Miller then we'll clean it up to make sure it still works," Jonah tells him as he turns back to the screens and studies them closely.

1830 HOURS
PRESENT-DAY
CONSTRUCTION TRAILER MAMMOTH LAKES, CALIFORNIA

"This is Leon," he says answering the phone.

"Leon, this is Aaron. I just got off the phone with Senator Douglas, he wants our help in taking out Colonel Miller. Evidently Miller took off with a new model of the suits and is on his way to Doyle's location."

"Yeah, that's what Mike told me. The SG operator on the ground there was Amy Leek, who I did not know was trained to operate those suits. Mike killed her but not before she told him what Miller was planning on doing," Leon explains.

"Yeah, we knew she had been operating during missions the past few years in the suit. Leon, listen to me; you must get them out of there now. There are two special forces teams heading there as we speak with orders to kill anyone near Miller. I got them to agree that anyone below the Devil's Bathtub they will let pass unharmed. They are to sweep the entire area above that and leave no trace they were there. That means bodies, shells, suits, and everything else," Aaron explains to him.

"I can't reach them as long as they are in that bunker. They are set to start towards the pickup zone in twenty minutes, I'll be able to contact them at that point," Leon replies.

"What kind of bunker are they in?" Asks Aaron.

"Jonah built himself a bunker up above the Devil's Bathtub," replies Leon.

There's a slight pause before Aaron answers, "That's interesting. Okay. Leon this is your operation, so I won't step on your toes but get your men out of there as soon as possible."

1845 HOURS
PRESENT-DAY
INSIDE JONAH'S BUNKER

"What in the hell are you girls up to?" Mike asks as he enters the main room of the bunker.

"We've got a plan that just may work," Doyle replies.

"Oh yeah, and what's that?" asks Mike.

Jonah holds up the suit, "This is one of our prototype suits from the 1970s, it's not as good as what Miller has on, but it may be good enough to keep him from seeing me. Two things though, one we need to get him to show himself and two, get him close enough to me."

"Sounds like you've got it all figured out but the doing it thing," Mike snaps.

"Well Mike, you can keep complaining or you can help me get this on. We are running out of time," Jonah tells him.

Mike walks over and helps Doyle put the suit on Jonah, it is stretchy enough to go on over his underwear and tee-shirt but not his

pants or jacket. The bottom of the pant legs has flaps that drop down over his boots and a strap that goes under his boot to hold them in place.

"That was not the best design for the feet, from behind you can see the bottom of my feet when I walk," explains Jonah.

"Considering this was used in the 1970s is still pretty damn impressive," responds Doyle.

"Okay, Doyle would you hand me that small round metal container in the bottom of the chest? That is the face paint, there is also a small brush in the chest as well," Jonah tells him.

"I sure will," Doyle replies, sliding over to the chest.

"How's your leg feeling?" Mike asks Doyle.

Doyle hands Jonah the paint and brush then answers, "The medication has kicked in so it's feeling okay. Good enough I feel for me to get off this damn mountain."

Before Mike could respond they hear and feel a sonic boom, "He's in the area," Jonah says as he is applying the face paint.

Mike looks up at the ceiling of the bunker, "I'd say he's heading to the site of the dead SG operator and it will not take him very long to track us here." He looks at his watch, "It's 1855 so that means in five minutes we're out of here, get your shit ready it's time."

Doyle grabs his backpack, "How can one of those suits break the sound barrier?" he asks Jonah.

"They don't...in theory. What these new suits are actually doing is going from this dimension to almost into the next. I will explain more of that to you at Edwards Air Force Base later," he replies then turns around, "Okay. Let's see if she's still working." He flips a switch on the backpack, and it starts making noises. There is a few sparks and cracks and then Jonah almost appears see through. His face glows for a second then it too appears see through. "She's still got it boys!" he yells.

He flips the switch again and the backpack shuts down. "I've got a plan boys. We exit the bunker and move to the west where we will find a ledge that dead ends at a cliff. There are a few trees just prior to this area that I can hide behind. You guys go out on the ledge like you are looking down below and hopefully Miller will enter the area. He will think he has you guys cornered then I will slip up behind him and insert the remote."

"So, you want us to be the bait uh? Why do you constantly like putting us in a situation where we have no way to escape if something goes wrong?" Mike asks him.

"What could go wrong?" Jonah asks laughing.

Mike walks over to the door to unlatch it, "It's time," he says pushing the rock out of the way as a blast of cold air rushes into the cave.

Jonah moves over to the computers, "One second, let me activate my security system so no one can open that door while I'm gone. I don't want some of this technology falling into the wrong hands."

As soon as the doorway is clear Mike and Doyle's phones start vibrating. Doyle pulls his phone out of his pocket after he exits the bunker. "It's from Leon, I'll call him," he says to Mike.

Jonah is the last to crawl out of the bunker. He pushes the rock back in front of the entrance and then reaches into a crack on the side of the bunker and opens a hidden panel. "I'll set the security code here and it takes my fingerprint to reopen this panel. That's it…we're all set."

Doyle walks over to both, "We've got to get moving guys and quick."

"What's up?" Mike asks.

"They're sending in two Special Operations Force (SOF) teams to remove Miller. We have to clear the area, or we'll be considered working with Miller," replies Doyle as he removes his trekking pole and unfolds it to use as a cane.

"Let's move to the West to get to our location to trap Miller," Jonah says.

"We don't have time for that Jonah! We move out now or the guys coming will for sure kill us." snaps Doyle.

"Did Leon say what they consider the area?" Mike asks.

"Anything above the Devil's Bathtub," Doyle replies pointing to the lake below their location. "You guys go and don't wait on me, I'll be right behind you moving as fast as I can," explains Doyle.

"Activate that suit so Miller won't see you, maybe one of us can

make it out of here," Mike tells Jonah.

Jonah flips the switch and disappears, with nightfall having set in he is completely invisible. The wind is still blowing over thirty miles per hour causing the trees to make noise helping the sounds from the suit go unnoticed. Mike is forty yards ahead of Doyle who is having a hard time moving on the rocky soil. He uses the trekking pole as a replacement for his injured leg. The wind keeps kicking up snow and hitting them in the face making seeing very far ahead impossible.

"You okay Doyle?" Mike yells back to him.

"I'm good, just keep going!"

After Doyle says that he hears what sounds like the wind coming towards them. He hears Mike grunt and sees him being lifted several hundred feet into the air then let go to free fall back to the ground. He hears Mike screaming as he drops behind a stand of trees and hears him hit the ground...then silence.

1915 HOURS
PRESENT-DAY
SAN FRANCISCO, CALIFORNIA

"Senator Douglas, come on in," The FBI director tells him.

"Thank you, sir."

"Tell me Senator, what's the status with Colonel Miller?"

"We have made an agreement with the Patriots that he is to be re-

moved. I've just been informed the two SOF teams are on the ground as we speak," the Senator explains.

"That's good Senator, tell me...how did you allow Miller to take off with that suit?"

The Senator laughs, "Bite-me. I do not work for you, bitch! You do not call me in here and then demand to know things you have no idea about. Who in the hell do you think you are? I was in this game back when you were still on your momma's tit!" The senator says as he pulls a cigar out of his suit pocket.

The Senator takes a few big draws on the cigar, "So, if there's nothing else Director. Tell your wife to give me a call sometime," he says, blowing smoke in the Directors face. "Like I said, I don't work for you…"

"No, but you do work for me!" A man says walking into the room from behind the Senator.

"Mr. Vice President, sir. I didn't know you were here," the Senator says standing up.

The Vice President walks up to the Senator, "Put that nasty-ass thing out now, Stanley. That will be all Director," he says to the FBI director as he walks around the desk and sits down. He sits there looking at the Senator until the Director leaves the room. "Tell me Stanley, what is it going to take for you to get your group in order?"

"What do you mean, sir?"

"Oh, come on Stanley. You know damn well what I am talking

about. First your group fumbles the ball with the Wolfgang kid and in the process, you end up awakening one of the country's finest soldiers. Who now, might I add, has joined the Patriots group. And that brings us to the present, where one of your guys steals a top-secret suit, kills four of our operators, and then kills your deputy director."

"Yes sir, but I'm in the process of getting rid of all the loose cannons," the Senator replies.

"This is your way of tying up loose ends. A maid found Agent Atkins body; do you know how hard that is going to be to keep that out of the press? Luckily, she did not enter the bathroom, she just turned and ran to call for help. We were able to find a drug addict prostitute nearby that we took and put in the bathroom and staged a murder suicide scene," explains the Vice President.

"I understand sir," the Senator says as four men walk into the room and start spreading plastic on the floor.

"I don't think you do Stanley. We are now forced to work with the Patriots to remove Miller," he tells him as the Senator starts to move restlessly in his chair looking back at the plastic on the floor.

"Now wait just a damn minute!" replies the Senator.

Two of the men walk over and jerk the Senator out of his chair and force him down on his knees on the plastic sheeting that is spread out.

"I'm a damn United States Senator you sons-of-bitches!" he yells.

"You were a senator...Stanley," says the Vice President.

One the men pushes him down on his face and places a gun to the back of his head.

“Wait! Wait! Let’s talk about this!” the Senator yells.

“Time to talk is over Stanley. Let them in,” the Vice President says to one of the men.

The man opens the door and walks two young girls into the room. “It’s a shame that you tried to force yourself onto these two beautiful girls and one of them killed you,” the Vice President tells him, handing one of the girls a 9mm.

“What in the hell are you talking about?” the Senator yells.

They walk the young girl over to the Senator, then place the barrel to his head.

“Wait!” he yells.

“Okay, sweetie go ahead and pull the trigger. He’s a really bad guy…it’s okay,” one of the men tells the girl.

“No! Wait!” Stanley yells

The girl pulls the trigger and the 9mm just clicks…

One of the men quickly escorts both the young girls from the room.

“Okay gentlemen, that’ll be all,” the Vice President says as everyone else turns and leaves the room.

“Smells like you shit your pants Stanley,” he says squatting down beside him. “This is your last warning, fix your group!”

The Vice President stands up and walks over to a mirror on the wall and straightens his tie. "And clean this mess up," he says as he leaves the room.

The Senator slowly rises onto his knees and he gasps for breath as he looks around the room.

The SOF teams start their assent up the mountain.

Leon sits tapping a pen on his desk as he watches real-time drone footage.

Chapter Nine:
MILLER TIME

1920 HOURS
PRESENT-DAY
NORTH OF THE DEVIL'S BATHTUB, CALIFORNIA

Doyle, squatting down beside a tree scans the area for movement when he sees snow fall from a tree off to his left. He aims his 9mm in that direction.

"What's wrong Anderson?" a voice from his left echoes through the mountains. "Are you afraid?" the voice says now coming from his right. Doyle turns and looks in that direction.

"Show yourself, Miller!" Doyle yells as he stands up slowly and starts heading south towards the lake.

"Come out and fight like a man, Miller!" he yells.

"Anderson you always surprise me on how stupid you really are. I'm shocked someone hadn't killed you by now," the voice says now coming from in front of him.

"Then come on out and kill me, Miller!" he yells moving towards the voice.

"What did you do with the old man wizard?" the voice asks now coming from behind Doyle.

"Your other operator fatally wounded him, he died!" Doyle yells.

"So, you're all alone and injured. This is going to be like shooting fish in a barrel," says the voice back on Doyle's left side.

"I know what you're trying to do Miller, it's not going to work. Like I said come on out and let's do this like men!" yells Doyle.

A strong gust of wind passes by Doyle and knocks him off his feet. Approximately thirty yards to Doyle's right two footprints appear in the snow. Doyle rolls to his left side and quickly fires four shots at the footprints. A few bright flashes light up the darkness and just for a second, he sees Miller standing there before the snow is kicked up and Miller disappears once again.

"You're going to have to do better than that Anderson!" Miller yells to him from the north of his location.

"Don't worry Miller, I intend to! I know you're the one that killed Bullseye!" Doyle yells.

Laughing echoes through the mountains, "If you would have just died like you were supposed to Anderson, you could have saved him," Miller says.

Doyle slowly gets to his feet and keeps moving south towards the Devil's Bathtub when he asks, "What's that supposed to mean?"

"You weren't supposed to survive the cornstalk mission. Who do you think wired that place to blow? I did! I knew you would go back to try and save those kids; my men were supposed to kill you. Who would have thought a few kids would save your ass!" Miller shouts from beyond the trees to Doyle's left.

"You're a sick bastard!" Doyle yells as he tries to keep moving.

Miller flies past Doyle clotheslining him as he passes, Doyle hits the ground and cuts his head above his left eye on a rock. He can feel the blood running down his cheek, "You going to fight like a man or keep hiding behind that suit?" he asks as he gets to his feet once more.

"Susan's not here to help you this time Anderson!"

Jonah stays inside the tree line as he watches Doyle limp along, "I've got to help him somehow," he says out loud stopping by a tree when he notices snow kicking up behind Doyle moving right at him. "Look out Doyle!" he yells.

Doyle drops to the ground just as Miller flies over him and lands thirty-five yards in front of him.

"So, the wizard is not dead!" Miller shouts as he scans the area for Jonah.

Doyle pulls himself up on his knees, aims his 9mm at Miller and fires four rapid shots. All four rounds hit their mark causing Miller to be visible for a few seconds.

Miller turns and looks at Doyle before slowly disappearing again. He lifts off the ground and flies to Doyle at a high rate of speed hit-

ting him in the face with both fists. Blood shoots into the air as Doyle slams onto his back feeling all the air in his lungs rushing out of his mouth.

"I'm going to enjoy killing you Anderson," Miller says from high above Doyle.

Doyle rolls over onto his stomach, desperately trying to catch his breath, "Come and get you some Miller," he says getting up on all fours and spitting blood out of his mouth.

"Where are you wizard?" Miller yells from the top of a nearby ledge looking below for Jonah.

Meanwhile, a few hundred yards south of their location the complete blackness is slowly breaking up as Mike slowly opens his eyes. He lays flat on his back looking up at a lone star shining bright, the image is crystal clear as if he could reach out and touch it. Behind the star he notices what looks like clouds starting to gather, as the clouds roll and softly come together, they grow larger. He watches as the tops of the clouds break away from each other forming the outline of people.

There are tens of thousands of what now looks to Mike to be warriors. He can see that the star is not a star but a crown being worn by what looks like a king sitting on his throne. Mike blinks several times and then tries to move but cannot move anything but his eyes. He can now see another person approaching on a white horse from behind the warriors as the masses move apart to open a path for the rider.

The white horse trots up to the right side of the king then turns broadside to Mike as the rider looks at Mike with eyes of fire. He can see that the rider is wearing several crowns and that the armor he wears has been dipped in blood. His name is written across his chest plate, but Mike cannot read the odd letters. The gap in the warriors now slowly closes behind the king and the rider.

"Who are you?" Mike whispers. He can see their heads moving but cannot see their faces, the colors are so vivid unlike anything he has ever seen before. To the left of the king, he sees what looks like a small circle start slowly spinning. Both the king and rider turn to look at the small whirlwind object as it spins faster and grows bigger. They turn and look back at Mike as he sees that there are now millions of warriors standing behind them.

He can hear their voices, but it is not a language he understands, it sounds to him as if they are singing. The whirlwind is now spinning so fast that he can see another world inside of it. Mike tries to see what the world is when he hears in his head, "It's not your time!" The rider of the white horse opens his mouth, a sword shoots out and lunges towards Mike...everything goes black again.

Mike opens his eyes and feels the pain throughout his body, he looks around and notices that he has sunk down into the ground about eight inches. There's moss and dead grass laying all over him, "I must have landed in some marsh near the lake," he says out loud. He sits up and rolls out of the hole facedown, "That hurt like shit," he whispers as he stands up.

"You don't see that every day," he says looking at what looks like a cookie cutter image of him in the soft ground. "Thank GOD it warmed up enough to thaw this part of the ground out."

He looks out across the Devil's Bathtub and sees the stars reflecting in the water, he looks up to the sky, "I'm not sure why you keep saving me but, thanks." He sees his backpack floating in the lake a few feet away from him. He grabs a dead tree limb laying nearby and fishes his backpack out of the water.

"Come out wizard," Miller yells.

Jonah slowly moves behind a larger boulder and looks over at Doyle who is struggling to get back on his feet. Doyle grabs his trekking pole and stands up as Miller appears landing between him and Jonah.

"Here I am, Anderson," Miller snaps holding his arms straight out.

Miller starts slowly walking towards him, "Tell me, how did you manage to get the Wolfgang kid away from the hospital?"

"Why do you care?" Doyle asks.

Miller laughs, "You know I will find your buddy Louis too. You can't hide him forever and when I do, I'm going to make him suffer."

Doyle wipes blood off his mustache, "What happened to you Miller? Or were you always screwed in the head?"

"Coming from the guy who was forced out of the army," Miller replies laughing. "You were lucky not to spend time in prison, Ander-

son."

"You beat the shit out of your wife, Susan's best friend. You hit her so hard her eye swelled shut. You got what you deserved!" snapped Doyle.

"Threw your perfect record away because you couldn't control your temper," Miller tells him.

"It was worth it. What was it...two teeth and four broken ribs?" he asks Miller.

"And you broke my left arm, jackass!" Miller responds.

"O'yeah, I forgot about the arm. You didn't even get a punch in, did you?"

Miller smiles at him, "No. But you helped me get my commission and you were kicked out."

"True, but I was allowed to keep doing my job as a civilian. The one regret I have is I should have let them prosecute me, that way you would have been kicked out for beating your wife. I would have gladly done a little time to keep you away from power," Doyle tells him.

"That never would have worked. Remember you jumped me on the golf course in front of our company commander," says Miller.

"That's right, I forgot there was an audience watching you get the ass beating of a lifetime," Doyle tells him laughing.

"It's my turn now Anderson. Except this time, you will not just get your ass kicked, I am going to kill you," Miller explains as he slowly

disappears.

Doyle starts walking towards the lake as snow flies into the air when Miller takes off. He stops and leans on a larger boulder to rest his leg when he feels something touch his shoulder.

"It's me Doyle," he hears Jonah say.

"Act like you don't hear me and try to draw him closer to this rocky area so he can't see my footprints," Jonah tells him.

Doyle places his hand in front of his mouth, "We've got to get the hell out of here or we're dead."

"I know," Jonah replies.

Doyle continues walking south as he moves where the wind has blown the snow away. The rocky surface causes him more pain every time he steps on the uneven ground.

"Where are you at Miller?" he shouts.

There is no response as he can now see the lake ahead, only problem is there is no route that is not snow covered. He stops and looks around when he sees a small glitter of light reflect off something behind a tree forty yards south of his location.

"Shit, they're here," he whispers.

Just as he starts to continue Miller grabs him from behind around the neck.

"Your time is up Anderson," Miller says as he appears holding a knife in his right hand. Doyle, so weak from his injuries he cannot

fight back, drops his trekking pole, and then tries to reach his pistol.

"Sorry brother, I'll take care of Susan for you," Miller tells him as he places the knife on his throat.

All of a sudden sparks fly and Miller steps back and drops the knife. He shakes and jerks, having no control on the suit he falls forward onto his knees. He pushes buttons on a keypad on his left forearm to no avail.

"Remember the word spoken before. That there shall be mockers in the last days who should walk after their own ungodly lusts!" shouts Jonah.

"The four angels that were bound in the great river Euphrates are loose!" Jonah screams up at the sky.

Doyle falls over onto his face and tries to continue crawling towards the lake.

Miller still jerking now tries to remove the suit as he feels the remote Jonah placed into the back of the suit.

"What have you done you son-of-a-bitch!" Miller yells.

"Here is wisdom. Let him that hath understanding count the number of the beast. For it is the number of a man and his number is six-hundred threescore and six!" Jonah shouts to Miller.

Jonah sees the special forces moving towards them. He looks at Doyle then turns to Miller and says, "Behold, I come as a thief. Blessed is he that watcheth and keepeth his garments, lest he walk naked and they see his shame!"

Jonah leaps on top of Doyle and they slide down between two boulders. He places the bottom of his feet on the side of one of the boulders to hide the part of him that is not invisible.

"Don't move, they're here," Jonah tells him as they both disappear.

Several more sparks fly as the suit malfunctions causing the jetpack to fire up. Miller flies high into the sky and then crashes on top of the mountain on what is called Graveyard Peak. The special forces race up towards the peak while a few stays behind.

"Sir, I thought I saw another man standing over here, but he's gone now," one of the operators says into his mic.

"Forget him. He's out of our kill zone sergeant, keep moving forward," the other operator responds.

Jonah watches until the operators are out of sight, "Come on Doyle, let's get out of here."

He helps Doyle up and hands him his trekking pole. Doyle again wipes blood from his mouth then says, "We've got quite a way to go to get to the pick-up point. I need more pain relief." He drops his pack and pulls out a syringe. He jabs the needle into his thigh above the knee and injects the morphine.

"That should get me there, unless I get in another fight," he tells the invisible Jonah looking around not seeing him.

"I'm here Doyle," Jonah replies from behind him.

As they start walking, they hear a large drone fly overhead, "Shits about to get real bud," Doyle says.

"I'm glad we're heading in the opposite direction," replies Jonah.

"Anderson! Anderson! This is not over!" a voice echoes from the mountain peak. Then the sound of gunfire drowns out the voice. The two guys keep walking without turning back and looking. Jonah deactivates the suit before it shuts down automatically from low battery life.

"We need to find Mike's body and take it with us. No man left behind," Doyle explains to him as he stops and shines his flashlight around looking.

"That'll make it hard for us to reach the helicopter carrying a body," Jonah replies.

"I don't care, I'm not leaving him here!" snaps Doyle.

"I think I can walk myself off this mountain," Mike says sitting on a fallen tree trunk off to their left.

"What the...how did you survive that fall?" Doyle asks.

"Soft ground and moss," says Mike.

Jonah walks over and pats him on the shoulder, "Glad you're okay Mike."

"Don't get all mushy, we still have to get off this mountain," Mike says standing up and putting his backpack on. "You coming ladies?" he asks as he turns and starts walking down the mountain.

"Right behind you," responds Doyle as a large explosion goes off from the top of Graveyard Peak followed by rapid machine gun fire.

The three guys pick up their pace trying to get away from the scene as fast as they can. "I don't want anyone seeing us near all that," Mike tells them, stopping to let both pass by him.

"Come in Mike, do you have a copy?" Leon asks over the radio.

Mike looks down at his radio, shocked that it stills works after the fall, then replies, "Roger-that, I copy,"

"I take it all three of you are clear of the Devil's Bathtub area?" asks Leon.

"We are. Maybe three-hundred yards south," Mike tells him.

"Great. Head to the Mono Creek Trailhead southwest of your location. I have a vehicle there to pick you guys up. Hide all your weapons before you reach this location. The guy there thinks you are just hikers and that Doyle fell and broke his leg. His name is Doug," explains Leon.

"Roger-that," Mike replies.

"Doug will take you to the Mono Hot Springs Resort just south of the pick-up zone. I've told him that you guys are being airlifted out, do not do any talking other than hi and thanks," Leon tells Mike.

"Will do. We are probably thirty minutes from there," says Mike.

"Ten-four. I'll meet you guys at Edwards Air Force Base in a few hours," Leon says.

"Roger-that, Mike out. Guys we have a ride to take us to the helicopter. He's waiting for us at the trailhead," he explains to them.

"Jonah, you need to get out of that suit," Doyle tells him.

Jonah drops his backpack and digs into it, "You're not going to believe this, guys."

"Let me guess, you forgot to pack your clothes," Mike says shaking his head.

"I remembered to put my jacket in here though," he tells Mike holding it up.

"Just put it on. Maybe no one will notice your pants," replies Doyle.

Jonah puts the coat on over the suit and the guys continue south to the pick-up point. Bright flashes light up the night from the fire fight that is going on behind them. As they get close to the trailhead, they stop to make sure none of their weapons are visible. Jonah reaches down and removes the flaps that cover his boots and places them in his backpack. Mike leads the way out of the forest onto the road when they see an old Ford Bronco setting there running.

"Are you Doug?" Mike asks walking over to the bronco.

"Yes sir, are you Mike, Corey, and Doyle?" he asks Mike, reading the names off a note in his hand.

"That's correct," replies Mike.

"One of you fellows is hurt?" Doug asks.

"I am. I think I blew out my knee," Doyle tells him.

Doug walks over to Doyle and looks at his leg, "Oh my. That's gotta

hurt like the dickens."

"Yes, it sure does," replies Doyle.

"What were you doing up yonder to cause you to hurt it?" asks Doug.

Doyle chuckles at his accent then replies, "I just lost my footing and twisted it."

"What's all that shooting about up there? Sounds like a war going on." Doug asks them as he looks up the mountain.

Mike walks over to him, "We're not sure what it is, that's one of the reasons we want to get out of here."

"I bet it's those gosh-damn game wardens. Those no-good turds are always screwing with someone," Doug tells them.

"Yeah, maybe that's it," Mike says, walking to the bronco.

"Y'all climb in, it's a short drive to the resort. By the way, what is up with this fellers' britches? Kind of looks like he's stuck in the forties." Doug asks them pointing at Jonah's pants.

"They are new space age heated pants," responds Jonah.

"That's what you call them, uh?" asks Doug climbing into the bronco.

Mike helps Doyle into the back seat, then he walks around and gets in the passenger seat. Jonah climbs in the back with Doyle, "I don't think my pants really look that bad…"

Doyle laughs, "Not at all brother, they're stylish."

The four guys head down the road to the resort.

Gunfire and bright flashes continue from the top of the mountain.

Chapter Ten:

GET TO THE CHOPPER

2045 HOURS
PRESENT-DAY
SOUTH OF MONO CREEK TRAILHEAD, CALIFORNIA

"These roads are four times slicker than snot on a doorknob," Doug tells Mike as they drive along at ten miles per hour.

Mike laughs and looks at him, "Just get us there in one piece."

"The temps are dropping fast so it may take us fifteen to twenty-minutes to get there guys. Plus, this old bronco does not handle like she used to," Doug says, fighting the steering wheel to keep the bronco in the center of the road.

Jonah leans over to Doyle, "You feel okay?"

"Yeah, I'm just very tired, going to shut my eyes for a bit," replies Doyle.

"Tell me Matt…" Doug starts before Mike cuts him off.

"My name is Mike."

"Oh, sorry Mike. Let me ask you something. Since you guys have been up in these mountains hiking, I am wondering, have you guys run into that bigfoot thing up there?" asks Doug.

"What's a bigfoot thing?" Mike answers his question with his own.

"You know what I'm talking about. A sasquatch or a Yeti. I saw one up north of here years ago," Doug says, looking over at him.

"No. We haven't seen any big feet or anything," Mike says rolling his eyes.

"You're not a believer in them are you, Matt?" Doug asks.

"Again. My name is Mike and no, can't say that I am."

Doug continues fighting the bronco on the slick roads when he looks at Mike. "They're wonderful creatures, big, and faster than green grass through a goose."

Mike stares out the passenger's side window when he whispers, "Lord, maybe you shouldn't have let me survive the fall."

"They also smell bad enough to knock a dog off a gut wagon," Doug says then starts laughing. "Huge boogers too! The one I saw stood at least nine-feet tall."

Mike looks at him, "Keep your mind on the road, thanks."

"Don't worry about that Mike, I ain't never had a wreck yet. Anyhow, back to my story. This bigfoot feller, he was squatting down trying to grab something out of the creek when I saw him. As luck would have it, I was upwind of him so he could not smell me. I

stood there watching him for...oh, I would say ten-minutes. I slipped behind a tree watching, at first I thought it was a man in a suit, but I soon could tell he didn't have the build of a man."

Doug looks over at Mike, "His face was a lot longer than a man's. Those eyes though, looked just like mine and yours. He fished there in that creek when suddenly, he stopped and looked up right towards me. I just about crapped my pants when he slowly stood up. I could see him sticking his nose up in the air trying to find where I was, just like an animal. In a flash he reached down, grabbed a rock, and threw it at the tree I was standing behind. That rock hit dead-center on the tree and exploded into dust."

"After the tree stopped rocking from the hit, I slowly peaked my head out to look at him again when he saw me and started growling. I could see him take a deep breath and swell his chest up when...the loudest scream, growl, whatever it was vibrated the tree I was touching. It sounded like a horn on a train but even louder. That bigfoot took one large step into the creek looking dead at me. He acted like he was about to launch himself at him when I tucked tail and ran like hell. I didn't stop until I was at least a mile away from that creek."

"The whole time I could hear him running alongside of me in the woods but far enough away that I could never see him." Doug stares out the windshield for a few minutes, then says, "If I never see another bigfoot that'll be okay with me."

Mike never says a word just sits there listening to him tell the story. He glances back at Jonah and Doyle a few times and notices that

Jonah is hanging on every word. Doyle has dropped his head over against the door and is slipping in and out of sleep. He can hear the guys talking but is only picking up every other word or so. He keeps hearing the word bigfoot as he finally falls asleep.

0930 HOURS
08 SEPTEMBER (DURING ALLEN WOLFGANG SAR)
DOYLE & SUSAN'S HOME

Doyle walks into his upstairs office and grabs a lighter out of his desk, one that has 'Operation Iraqi Freedom' stamped on it. He and Bullseye had several dozens of these made back in 2005 with their unit's shield on the front and Operation Iraqi Freedom on the back. Mounted on the opposite wall in a glass case is the one Bullseye had in his pocket that fateful night.

"I bet that hot shower felt good?" Susan says to Doyle as he comes down the stairs.

"Yes, it did," he says walking into the kitchen with his cell phone in hand.

"Here you go, babe, four scrambled eggs and bacon," she says, sitting his plate on the breakfast bar.

As they finish eating, they notice Barry pulling into the driveway, "I guess he wants to go to the briefing with me."

Doyle grabs his gear and walks outside to his truck when he notices Gunner's silhouetted outline looking at him from the upstairs bed-

room window. Doyle smiles, salutes him, and climbs into the truck as Barry walks over to the passenger's door.

Doyle glances at his dad, "You have your gun on you?"

"Never leave home without it. Hell, I never stay home without it," Barry responds laughing as he climbs into Doyle's truck.

After their laughter ends Barry looks over at him, "I need to tell you some things."

"Okay," says Doyle. "What kind of things?"

"Well - I've seen things in these mountains. Things I could not explain but things I saw. That SAR in the late sixties was the first - the one where we never found that young boy. Then again in the mid-seventies, on the SAR where we did not find that teenage girl. The last time was in 1991 during the SAR after the plane crash on Long Drive Ridge."

"What kind of things are you talking about dad?"

Barry looks straight ahead thinking. "The only way I can describe it is that - is that it was a spirit, or something. I call it the devil. It was like looking at a highway in the middle of the summer, you know, when you can see those squiggly lines coming off it and the light and colors are all blurred and bent. But this thing had a body - enough of one to run and climb trees."

"Well…that's interesting. Because I saw something like that just the other morning, up in a tree."

"Did you shoot it?"

"Nope. I was trying to figure out what I was seeing and then it disappeared."

Barry looks over at him. "I've been doing some reading on people that go missing in the forest and are never found. There is this fellow out west that is researching a certain category of these missing people. He came here several years back to interview me about a case in the mid-seventies. A lot of the things he mentioned I've witnessed first-hand."

Barry pauses, "The details make no sense. Young kids and even elderly people walking crazy distances. Or they just vanish, and they are never found - not even a body. You should investigate it Doyle. I'd be willing to bet you've encountered some of the same things."

The two of them ride quietly as Doyle pulls out onto highway 74. They head east on 74 for a few miles, and then as Doyle takes exit 64 Barry continues.

"I was taking this very exit in 1984, when I spooked something. It was eleven at night and I had been down in Cowee at the site of an accident. It was foggy and I was very tired. I pulled off the highway and was getting ready to break so I could turn left on Highway 19."

"There was something black on the shoulder. As I got closer, the thing stood up on two feet and took one big step into the woods. This thing was huge, but I never saw its face. Instead of turning left, I turned right, because the road loops back around and the trees were not as thick as they are today plus, I wanted to see it again. After I came around the curve, I stopped and turned on my spotlight. I

didn't see anything, so I stepped out of the squad car."

"And?" Doyle asks.

"There was this horrible stink. I mean, it watered my eyes. I felt like I was being watched and it was so quiet that I started to feel uneasy. I slowly reached into the car and turned my flashing lights on." Barry pauses as Doyle stops to turn left on highway 19.

He looks out the window before continuing. "See that old fence right there? Back then there were no trees in it, it was clean, and you could see way out into the field with the only trees being those between the two roads. Anyway, as I started walking towards the tree line, I pulled out my weapon with my right hand and had my flash-light in my left. Suddenly I felt so sick to my stomach that I almost went down to my knees."

Doyle listens as he turns and continues towards Bryson City. "What then Dad?"

"What?" Barry asks.

Doyle laughs, "What happened next, you felt sick and then…"

"Oh. Like I was saying, I almost puked right there on the side of the road. When suddenly there was this scream or growl so loud, I could feel it in my chest. I headed back to the car, got in, and started backing out of there. I backed up all the way out to Bear Cove Road across highway 19 with my lights still flashing, I was afraid to turn around until that point. I floored the gas pedal and squealed my tires, I was so shook up that I forgot to turn my flashers off until I was

almost to town. I guess it was one of those Bigfoot creatures. Hell, I don't know."

"It was a different kind of uneasy feeling compared to that devil thing; this was more a fear for my well-being, you know like right before a gun fight. The devil thing was not like that, it was more of an evil type feeling...one that keeps you up at night," Barry tells him.

"Bigfoot? You never told me! Dammit, Dad, holding back information on me. Geez!" Doyle says, laughing.

"I didn't want to scare you from going into the mountains. I read somewhere that Bigfoot emits infrasound if someone gets too close to them. I'm assuming that's what it did to me to cause that sudden sickness feeling," Barry explains.

"Yeah, I've heard that before," Doyle smiles shaking his head.

"My Dad saw Bigfoot and didn't tell me for thirty years..."

2100 HOURS
PRESENT-DAY
MONO HOT SPRINGS RESORT, CALIFORNIA

"I didn't tell you what?" Jonah asks Doyle.

Doyle looks up at him and smiles, "Was I talking in my sleep?"

Jonah softly laughs, "That you were but it was just mumble until that last part."

"What do you do here at the resort?" Mike asks Doug.

"I'm the maintenance man for the cabins and everything," he replies to Mike.

They pull just past the small cafe and then stop by the bath house. "We've been given the okay for the helicopter coming to get you boys to land in our tourist pasture," Doug tells them pointing to the pasture on the other side of the road.

"Doyle, we need to start for the helicopter," Jonah tells him as he gently shakes him because Doyle as drifted off to sleep again.

"Okay, I'm ready brother," replies Doyle.

"It was nice meeting y'all," Doug says to them as they exit the bronco.

Mike hands him a one-hundred-dollar bill, "Thanks for the ride partner."

They walk around to the front of the bronco when they hear the helicopter coming in for a landing.

"You good to walk a few hundred yards to the helicopter?" Mike asks Doyle.

"I'm good," Doyle tells him, gritting his teeth from the pain. "I walked in here, I'm damn well going to walk out of here."

"Roger-that," responds Mike.

The Blackhawk helicopter sets down in the pasture, kicking up snow causing an almost whiteout for a few seconds. The resort is noticeably quiet with only a few guests in one cabin, it looks like a post-

card with snow cover roofs. Smoke slowing rising out of a chimney from the cafe as the sound from the helicopter disrupts the silence.

Mike looks back and sees Doug standing beside the bronco leaning on the hood watching. He then looks up to the mountain top and notices that it is black, the fight must be over, and the once proud Colonel is dead. Jonah walks beside Doyle just in case he needs help crossing through the pasture to their ride. Two soldiers jog up to the guys and assist Doyle to the chopper.

"Good to meet you, Anderson," one of the soldiers says to him.

"Same here," replies Doyle.

They help Doyle into the Blackhawk and then Jonah climbs in and takes a seat across from him. Mike pulls himself up into the helicopter then looks back at Doug, who is now taking pictures with his phone.

"That's going to be a problem," he tells one of the soldiers.

"Yes, sir. No worries sir," the soldier tells him as he grabs a small device. He points it at Doug and a small dot, like a laser pointer, appears bouncing around near the area where Doug is standing. As soon as he gets the dot on Doug's phone the soldier presses a button on the device. "That phone is fried now," he tells Mike.

"Good, I didn't want to see our pictures on the internet tomorrow," Mike tells him as they slide the door closed.

As they lift off the ground, Mike looks down at Doug who is smacking his phone and looking at it in disgust. Doug looks up at the

Blackhawk and sees Mike in the window flying him the bird.

"You dad-gum hippy!" yells Doug as the Blackhawk flies out of sight over the mountain.

"Gentlemen, we'll arrive at Edwards Air Force Base in approximately twenty-minutes. We have a medic on board to assist you in anyway. Good to have you back on my helicopter Master Sergeant Anderson," the pilot says.

Doyle looks into the cockpit, "Warrant Perkins? Is that you?"

"Yes, it is. Been a long time since Operation Desert Storm in Iraq, I heard a few weeks ago you had joined us. Welcome aboard Doyle," Perkins says to him.

"Thanks," Doyle replies as the medic sits down beside him.

"Sir, I'm going to start an IV and then I'll look at your leg, okay?"

"Yes, that's fine," replies Doyle.

The medic helps Doyle out of his long sleeve shirt and pants then helps him lay back on the bench. "Okay, sir. Let's get this IV going. This will sting a little."

"That's okay. I've been through this plenty of times," Doyle says.

After the medic starts the IV, he removes the knee brace from Doyle's leg. He inspects his leg, rubbing his hands up and down his shin and bending his knee. "Sir, I have a better brace for your knee and upper shin. I feel a break in your fibula, I do not think I will need to set it, but I will try before I put the brace on. As far as the knee, it

feels screwed up but without an Xray we won't know for sure."

"Do what you need to sergeant," Doyle tells him.

He grabs a hold of Doyle's leg and tries to set it, he places the brace on it and tightens it up and then grabs the knee brace and tightens it, "That should hold everything in place until you can get it fixed."

"Thank you," replies Doyle.

"Okay, Mike, let me check you out really quick. You haven't been this bad looking in years," the medic tells him.

"You guys worked together before?" Doyle asks.

"Of course, we have, all of these guys are part of the Patriots group," Mike tells him.

"We're the rescue team for North America. We went on alert as soon as you and Mike hit the ground in Nevada," the medic tells him as he checks Mike's pulse.

"Doyle, we are the group that you will take over very soon. We work for you," Perkins tells him.

Doyle nods his head as he watches the medic check Mike.

"He took a one-hundred-foot cannonball onto the ground," Jonah chimes in.

Mike looks over at him, "Nobody asked you...Corey!" he snaps.

"Excuse me, geez."

"Where are you guys based?" Doyle asks the medic.

"Fort Campbell, Kentucky," he replies and then turns to Mike. "I want you to get checked over really good as soon as we get to Edwards to make sure you don't have any internal bleeding from that fall.

"I will, thanks."

"Corey, do you want me to check you out?" the medic asked.

"No, I'm good. Call me Jonah please. I'm not soft like these guys," He says laughing.

The guys sit quietly as they continue flying south. Jonah slides over to the window when he sees the lights of Edwards Air Force Base. "Every time I fly in here it reminds me of when I was younger, and we were testing the space shuttle in this very air space."

He sits there staring out the window before he continues, "That program made this place famous in the seventies and eighties. If people only knew what they cannot see, that's going on here."

"You worked on that program Jonah?" Doyle asks.

"Yes, I did. I also worked on the Apollo program in its latter years. But the shuttle program still holds a special place in my heart. I understand why they moved the landings to Florida, but I wished that part remained here."

The pilot comes over their headsets, "Gentlemen, we're starting our approach to Edwards. Should be on the ground shortly. We're landing at the south base, across the runway from the main base."

"Near the hangar they commissioned the B2-Bomber when I was

here in the nineties," Doyle says sitting up looking out the window.

"Why were you here?" Jonah asks him.

"We were heading to do some top-secret training and stopped here for a week to work with a group of Marines that had a camp across the lakebed east of here. We ended up playing golf every day and training at night. They have a nice golf course here on base, Muroc lake or something like that," explains Doyle.

Mike looks over at them, "That number four hole is a bitch, and I don't like hole twelve either, unfair par-three."

"I don't remember much about it, other than it was always windy," Doyle tells him.

Mike smiles, "The wind blows so much the trees grow leaning to the east. I had a hole-in-one on number seventeen a few years ago and I've also hit the pin on number eight three times now, but it won't go in."

"Sounds like you've got some game," Doyle says.

"Yeah, I used to have," replies Mike nodding his head.

Jonah reaches over and taps Doyle on the arm, "Once we enter the underground base, your life will never be the same."

"I didn't know they had an underground base," Doyle replies, sounding confused.

Jonah sits back up straight, "Exactly."

Doyle looks at Mike and holds his arms out with his palms towards

the roof in a what the hell kind of reaction.

Mike just shrugs his shoulders and winks at him.

The Blackhawk slows down and starts dropping to the ground.

Doyle looks out the window rubbing his chin and thinking about what Jonah just told him.

Chapter Eleven:

MOJAVE DESERT

2130 HOURS
PRESENT-DAY
EDWARDS AIR FORCE BASE

"Welcome to Edwards, Doyle," Jonah tells him as he helps him off the Blackhawk.

"Thanks buddy," Doyle says grabbing his hand.

"Doyle, are you good to walk?"

"Yes, this brace feels so much better," he tells Jonah as they follow Mike into a nearby hangar. Doyle turns and watches the Blackhawk lift off the ground and fly out of sight to the west.

"Doyle, come on in, the doors are getting ready to close," Mike tells him as a warning alarm starts beeping. Doyle steps in but still looking outside, "What are those lights to the south that look to be hanging in the air?"

Jonah walks up to him. "That's Mountain High ski resort, many

people think it's an UFO the first time they visit Edwards."

"Yeah, I remember that now," Doyle replies.

"Come on, let's get going. There are a lot of things I want to show you. This hangar wasn't here back in February 1954," Jonah explains.

"What happened in 1954?" Doyle asks.

Jonah stops at the top of a set of stairs leading down, "President Eisenhower came here to meet with a small group of extraterrestrials. This place was called Muroc Airfield back then, he came to this very set of stairs," Jonah says to him pointing at the steps.

The three men start down the stairway with Mike leading the way. "Back then the steps just led to a series of bunkers but in the sixty-plus years since, we have built an entire underground base and city," Jonah tells Doyle.

After two flights they stop by a door and Jonah unlocks it, "This is the very room where Eisenhower met with the aliens. This is also the actual door that one of the aliens stood guard at," explains Jonah as he opens the door. "The table and chairs are also the ones they used. Take a few minutes to look at the pictures on the wall," he tells Doyle.

"Are you screwing with me?" Doyle asks him.

"Absolutely not!" snapped Jonah.

Doyle walks over and looks at the pictures hanging on the wall. He sees President Eisenhower standing in between two blonde haired pale men. Their lips have no color at all and there is no sign of facial hair. "What did they want?" Doyle asks.

"They wanted to sign a treaty with the United States, in return they would assist us in our spiritual development. But the one condition was that we had to voluntarily stop our nuclear programs, which Eisenhower refused," explains Jonah.

Doyle looks over at Mike, "Is he pulling my chain?"

"No, he's not. If this is too much for you to comprehend, I would suggest you do not go any further. Wouldn't want your girly emotions shook up," replies Mike.

Jonah walks back to the doorway, "It's okay Doyle, you're not the first one to feel this way. There's a couple of projects that the government ran that you could read about when you have the time. Project Sigma and Project Plato. Eisenhower had another meeting in 1955 with a different group of aliens at Holloman Air Force Base in New Mexico, however, those pictures were destroyed. That meeting ended up with a treaty being signed but the aliens deceived Esienhower and there's been trouble ever since."

The group exits the room and walks to a nearby elevator, "There's a group that played a role in the 1955 meetings that we believe was the origins of the Shadow Government. That group has been called the Majestic Twelve," Jonah tells him as he enters a code into the elevator panel. "That group was formed in 1947 but many believe that the group is not real, just a hoax to throw everyone off their scent."

After they enter the elevator Jonah presses another button then turns to Doyle, "We've only scratched the surface my friend. When these doors open your life as you have known it will change forever.

One other thing, when I use the word alien, I am not talking about someone from outer space. I'm talking about someone from another dimension or realm."

Doyle doesn't respond, just stares at Jonah as he feels the elevator start to move downward.

"Even though they deceived Esienhower, we did gain a lot of expertise in their advanced technology. The space program was an area we used their technology and in the stealth programs. And of course, the invisible suits," Jonah tells him as they ride the elevator.

"So, all the talk about reverse technology is actually a fact uh?" Doyle asks.

"And then some," replies Jonah as the elevator doors start to open.

Doyle sees what looks like a city with paved sidewalks, shops run in a line on his left while train tracks run along on the right. On the other side of the train tracks is a rock wall with windows spaced out perfectly running as far as he can see.

After they step out, he turns and looks back to his right and sees a large door opening leading to an aircraft hangar. He sees at least fifty aircraft lined up with maintenance technicians working on them. Several he recognizes, the F-117 stealth fighter, several F-16 fighting falcons, the F-22 raptor, the SR-71 blackbird, and a U-2 dragon lady.

What are those? I have never seen that before, and that looks like one of the Space Shuttles sitting in the back, Doyle thinks to himself. As he turns to follow the guys he asks, "What are those aircraft for?"

"What aircraft?" Jonah asks him then turns and winks at him.

"That's outside our purview Doyle," Mike responds, walking up to a shop that has 'SECURITY' on the door.

"Hey, Larry. How's it going?" Mike asks the man behind the counter.

"It's going very good, Mike. Hey, Jonah, who do we have here?" Larry asks looking at Doyle.

Jonah puts his arm around Doyle, "This is Doyle Anderson our newest recruit."

"Holy-shit...I've heard a lot about you, Anderson. Happy to meet you, sir," he says holding out his hand.

"Thanks, Larry. Good to meet you too," Doyle says shaking his hand.

Larry reaches into a drawer and pulls out a sheet of paper. He fills it out and motions for Doyle to stand behind a line on the floor. "Let's get your picture taken so we can get you a badge."

There is a flash then Doyle can hear a computer start processing the information. Larry walks over and picks up a round device that is hooked to the computer. "Okay, if you'll please place your right thumb in here, I'll finish it up."

After Doyle sticks his thumb inside, Larry closes it over his thumb. Doyle can feel small electrical shocks as he stands there looking at Larry. The computer makes several beeping noises then the device pops open.

"Alrighty. Now, if you would lad, place your thumb on this scanner and look at that computer screen," Larry tells him.

Doyle walks over and places his thumb on the scanner and then notices that his picture and information has come up on the computer monitor.

"That's your badge, your right thumb. The program compared your DNA with the DNA we have on file for you, it confirmed that it was a match. Then it imprinted your badge under your skin. Only special readers can read it. Also, many people have asked if we implanted a chip into you, the answer is no. We do not need a chip to track you anymore, we track you by your DNA signature. Unfortunately, that is outside your purview and I cannot explain it any further."

Doyle stares at his thumb, "Okay, thanks, I guess."

The door to the security office swings open, "Glad you guys made it in one piece," Leon tells them. "Boy you guys are a rough looking bunch. Who dressed you Jonah?" Leon asks laughing. "Come on guys let's get you some clean clothes," he says holding the door open. They walk out of the office and notice a four-seat golf cart parked there.

"Climb on gentlemen," Leon tells them as he climbs in behind the steering wheel.

After the three men are seated in the golf cart Leon starts driving, "I'll take you guys to one of the locker rooms. Mike and Jonah have lockers there and Doyle, I've had the guys set you one up by theirs also. There is a whole wardrobe waiting for you, Doyle."

"Sweet, thanks brother," Doyle replies.

They drive a short distance making one left turn when Leon pulls up to two large double doors. "This is it, after you guys get cleaned up, meet me over there," Leon says pointing at an Amtrak coach car that is converted into a cafe.

The guys go through the doors to the locker room and Mike motions for Doyle to follow him, "Down this way. Jonah's locker is on the opposite side because he's a scientist," he explains leading him to a row of wooden lockers.

"Is this Mahogany wood?"

"Yes, it is. You have four lockers in this corner, each of the lockers have a thumb reader on them, so only you can open them. There are only twelve of us that use this area, you are the twelfth," Mike tells him.

"Very nice set up," replies Doyle.

"Also, all the shower stalls have benches, so you'll be able to sit down without causing that leg anymore stress. Outside each shower are all the towels and soap you need. After you get dressed, you will need to put on a lab coat and safety glasses," Mike explains.

Doyle opens all four lockers and notices that each has different items inside. There is one with several sets of clothing, one with personal hygiene items, one with shoes and boots, and one with lab coats and personal protective equipment. "This is very nice," he whispers to himself.

After showering and getting dressed, Doyle puts on a lab coat and safety glasses and walks back out into the tunnel. He sees Mike and Jonah standing outside the cafe waving at him. Still using his trekking pole for stability, he walks down to the cafe and enters the main entrance.

"Come on over and have a seat. They serve the best coffee in the world here," Leon says standing up holding his hand out.

Doyle walks over and sits down then the rest of the guys take a seat.

"Okay, guys, let me go over a few things." Leon says. "We were able to retrieve the other necklace device that Mike hung on a tree. One of our small drones flew in and picked it up. Our main objective was to bring you back here Jonah, glad to see that you didn't resist that effort."

"I felt resistance was futile," Jonah replies.

"That it would have been. Second, one of the SG operators was eliminated along with one suit. That leaves them now without a functioning suit. Miller showed up with a new prototype-suit, which was destroyed. However, Miller's body has not been found yet," Leon tells them.

"Say what?" Mike asks.

Leon frowns, "They can't find his remains. He removed the suit before it self-destructed but there's no way, he could have survived all that fire power that rained down on that mountain."

"Don't put it past that crazy bastard. I've seen him escape things

that would have killed me and you," explains Doyle.

"I hear you. Anyway, the team on the mountain will continue the search through the morning and clean the site up, if no sign of him is found they'll just move on."

"Is it possible that Miller had another suit to change into and escape?" asks Mike.

Leon shakes his head, "There is no other suit for him to use. The SG is out of suits, there are no more except the two we use and that old relic that Jonah has. No one came in to rescue him either, the airspace is still shut down and there are four other teams limiting access to that location. This is one of the largest operations we have ever run state-side. Plus, the SG wants him taken out too...we just don't know."

Doyle leans back in his chair, "He's alive, I'll bet you money."

"Even if he is, he'll have to go into hiding with the SG looking for him. Okay, that is all I have gentlemen. I understand they want to show you around this facility, or at least what you're allowed to see Doyle." Leon says standing up. He shakes their hands and then turns and walks out of the cafe. He climbs on the golf cart, waves at the guys, then drives out of sight.

"This coffee is amazing. Where are these beans grown?" Doyle asks.

"That's classified," Mike replies.

"Doyle, are you ready to be blown away?" Jonah asks him.

Doyle takes one last sip of the coffee, "Sure, I can't imagine you

have anything else to show me that's going to surprise me."

"Don't bet on it," snaps Mike.

"We'll go through the East-wing for now, then we'll loop back around through the North-bay to catch the northbound train at 0000 hours. It'll take us north to California City where we both live," explains Jonah.

"Does everyone that works here live there?" asks Doyle.

Jonah stands up and walks over to a trash can, "No, about half do, the other half live in Palmdale, California. There is also a southbound train, that's the tracks you saw when we entered the tunnels."

"Why do you call them tunnels?" he asks Jonah.

"That's what they are. There is a spider web of them under the desert floor, they started drilling them out in the early fifties. They stretch for many miles, mostly for the trains with the bulk of the usable areas under Edwards Air Force Base. Deep enough to withstand one of those bunker-buster bombs."

"That's crazy. How do they get the aircraft down here?" Doyle asks.

"Good question, Doyle. There is a section of the dry lakebed that lowers down with the aircraft on it. It is only done at night and with our scrambler devices to keep enemy satellites from seeing," explains Jonah.

"But that is…" Mike starts before Doyle cuts him off.

"Is outside my purview!"

Mike points at him, "Bingo!"

"So far, the areas we have been in is known as our commons area. You will find several restaurants here, plus all the locker rooms and the main hospital. PPE is not required here but it is in the rest of the facility. Let's walk to the East-wing," Jonah tells them as he starts walking towards a check in station.

They walk up to the checkpoint with several revolving gates, "Place your thumb in the scanner then just walk through the gate and through the metal detector," Mike says.

After they exit the metal detector, Jonah holds open a door for them to enter. Doyle sees a long tunnel with offices or rooms on both sides.

"This is the East-wing, the main tunnel is one-mile long with one-hundred cells or labs on each side. This is where most of the DNA research is done along with telepathic studies," Jonah explains as they walk down the center aisle of the main tunnel.

As they reach the halfway point of the tunnel, Doyle suddenly stops and bends over.

"What's wrong?" Mike asks him.

"I'm not sure I just all of a sudden felt very sick and dizzy."

"I know what it is, hang on just a second," Jonah tells them as he walks over to one of the cells and opens the door. Doyle hears Jonah speaking in a language he has never heard, then Jonah closes the door and returns.

"You should start to feel better now," he tells Doyle.

"How could you possibly know that?" Doyle asks as he sits on a nearby bench.

Jonah smiles, "You were just hit with infrasound my friend. I asked our associate to stop and he agreed he would."

"Your associate? What are you talking about?" he asks Jonah in a demanding tone.

"Oh, brother here we go," Mike sighs as he sits down beside Doyle.

"Yes, one of our associates. He is from Syria, Mount Hermon to be exact," replies Jonah.

"Mount Hermon... from the Bible? That Mount Hermon?"

"That's correct," Jonah says.

"You mean his family is from there, right?"

Jonah shakes his head, "No, he is from there. And his family too."

Doyle sits there for a few minutes until his belly stops rolling, "So, a Syrian has the ability to use infrasound uh?"

Jonah turns and looks at him, "I never said he was a Syrian."

"Will you just tell him so we can keep moving, I'd like to get to bed before the sun comes up," snaps Mike.

"Okay, I will. He is what many would call a Nephilim or a Watcher. His ancestors descended from Heaven to Mount Hermon. He is half flesh man and half angelic being. He and his type have been in hiding for thousands of years and we were lucky enough to convince him to work with us, in return we guarantee his safety," Jonah explains.

"I thought Mount Hermon was where Jesus was transfigured, I've never heard about this," says Doyle.

"It is the same place. But it is also where the Fallen Angels touched down. I believe that's why it was later used for the transfiguration of Jesus...there's something about that location we just don't understand," Jonah says as he turns away from the two guys on the bench.

"Can I meet him?" Doyle asks.

"Absolutely not. There are only two of us allowed in that room, the door I opened only leads to a waiting area. He is inside another room that leads deep into the earth. If you even looked at him, you would probably end up sick," explains Jonah.

Doyle looks at Mike who is staring at the floor, "What do you think about this?"

"I don't. Can we get moving now, please?" Mike asks Jonah.

"One last thing, Doyle. Most people that have ever seen him or the others like him, call them Bigfoot. Okay, we can move along now," Jonah says walking away from them.

"I'm not sure who is the craziest. Him, or me for listening to him," Mike tells Doyle as he gets up to follow Jonah.

Doyle laughs out, "Just when I thought I've heard it all, what's next, the wolfman?"

"That's outside your purview," Jonah yells back to him.

"Of course, it is," he yells.

"I've never seen him either, I think he's full of crap myself," Mike says as they speed up to catch Jonah.

"You'll notice that the tunnel narrows up ahead, that is the connector tunnel to the North-wing. It was designed this way in case there ever was a breach of one of the wings, they could close off the connector hallways to secure the other wings. That way the entire complex would not be compromised," Jonah tells them.

The narrow hallway runs for about two-hundred yards then stops at another checkpoint, except this one has four guards and two service dogs on duty.

"Gentlemen how are we this evening?" one of the guards asks.

"We're doing great, thanks," replies Mike.

"Guys, if you would walk through our machines one at a time so we can check you out. Thanks," another guard explains.

A third guard meets them at the exit, "Okay gentlemen, you are clear to proceed."

The fourth guard walks up to Mike, "I'm guessing you know that you need to visit the doctor soon? Looks like you have a small amount of internal bleeding."

"First thing in the morning, Major," Mike replies.

There is a loud buzzer sound and one of the doors to the North-wing starts to open.

Jonah leads the way then turns back to Mike and Doyle, "Right this

way."

"He's enjoying this way too much," Mike whispers.

"He looks like a child in a candy store," Doyle says.

As they enter the North-wing they notice a whole lot more people moving around working. This wing is considerably larger than the East-wing in width, it also looks to be several levels. Doyle walks over to a handrail and looks down what looks to be a few hundred feet. There are several disc-shape crafts sitting down below.

"Okay, what is this wing used for?" he asks.

Jonah and Mike walk over beside him and also look down below. Jonah puts his arm around Doyle then says, "This my friend is the real area-51."

Doyle slowly turns and looks at him after one of the disc-shape crafts lifts off the floor and slowly flies out of sight, "How do those flying machines exit?"

Jonah laughs, "There are launch tubes that exit in many places some are in the desert, some are at the bottom of lakes, and some are even in the bottom of the ocean."

Mike pats Doyle on the back, "This is not outside your purview but, we need to get moving if we're going to catch the last train north. You're staying at my house tonight in California City. Then first thing in the morning I have a doctor's appointment and you have a flight to catch. They are flying you to Fort Bragg to get that leg repaired."

Doyle turns to follow him, "Sounds good."

The three guys head towards the train station.

Doyle tries to understand what he has seen tonight...but he soon will have no choice but to do so.

Chapter Twelve:

TRYING TO GET HOME

2345 HOURS
PRESENT-DAY
NORTH TRAIN STATION – UNDERGROUND BASE

"We can go ahead and board, but the train won't depart until exactly zero-hundred hours," Mike tells Doyle.

The three guys board the train and Mike leads them to a private cabin. The small cabin has four luxury captains-chairs that face the middle of the room. There is one large window and a small bar on the wall with the door.

"Why would you need a bar just going to California City? It's what, a ten-minute ride?" asks Doyle.

"This train goes all the way to Northern California. Just west of California City it comes to the surface and uses the existing rails to the north," Mike tells him as he takes a seat and reclines the chair back.

"It just exits out of the tunnel and into the desert?" asked Doyle.

Mike lets out a laugh, "No. There is a heavily armed train station that is built into the side of a mountain where it comes to the surface."

"I see. Does the south train come to the surface too?"

"No, it never did. But it makes a large loop under the desert. It runs to Palmdale then east to Victorville and then back to the underground base. They wanted to add a line to Barstow, but they would have had to cross a few fault lines, so they never did. The bulk of the staff comes in from that south train, with most of the military special ops teams coming in from the north," Mike tells him.

"All aboard for the zero-hundred north-bound train to Cal-City," A recorded voice comes over the intercom system.

Doyle sees a few people heading for the train, "Not a lot of people catching the train," he says to Mike.

"No, most of the shifts run from nine to five. We only run two shifts here, 0900 hours to 1700 hours and then 2100 hours to 0500 hours. Our maintenance works 1300 hours to 2100 hours and then 0100 hours to 0900 hours, that is why this train runs at zero-hundred hours. It picks up maintenance personnel to get them here by 0100 hours," Mike explains.

"Interesting," Doyle says as he turns to Jonah. "Hey, you said earlier that only you and another person were allowed in that room. What did you mean by that?"

Jonah, sitting there with his eyes closed pauses a minute before

answering him. “You’re a religious man, right?”

“I am... most of the time.”

Before Jonah can continue the recording blasts again, “Last call for the north-bound train to Cal-City.”

Once the recording stops Jonah continues, “Well, you see. That dimension and this one cannot coexist, that is why GOD always used a burning bush or an ass to communicate with man. These suits that you have seen are not invisible in the fact that you cannot see them. They are invisible to you because they enter that dimension you cannot see.”

“Remember the Biblical story of Belshazzar’s feast when the hand appears and then writes on the wall, mene, mene, tekel, upharsin? That hand came from that dimension,” Jonah explains.

Doyle nods his head, “Interesting.”

“Quantum physics is just beginning to understand how all of this works. However, we have known for decades how it works, with the help of our Watcher friend. I’ll throw you a curve ball now, aliens are from that dimension and not outer space,” he tells Doyle as he looks at him before continuing.

“For whatever reason, a very small selection of people can interact with or even see beings from that dimension. Our associate knows that, and he can sense which one of us can look at him, he’s half and half - our dimension and the other,” explains Jonah.

“The doors are now closing. Enjoy your trip to Cal-City,” the re-

cording says as they feel the train start to move.

"So, he only found two of you that can enter?" Doyle asks.

"No. There were six of us, but the others have since passed away. The other person is already ninety years old, and I'm not far behind. Also, that's why certain people see them in the forest, and some don't," Jonah tells him.

Doyle nods his head again, "I see," he says as he sits back to enjoy the short trip to California City.

"Jonah, just so you know. You'll have round the clock surveillance until we're certain you won't try that shit again," Mike tells him with his eyes closed.

"I understand, Mike."

The train pulls out of the station and heads towards their destination. The tunnel has no lighting, the only light inside the cabin are the small led lights that run along the floor on each bench. There is nothing to see through the window as it appears to be painted with black paint, the only way to tell that the train is moving is from the slight shakes and bumps along the trip.

"Please remain seated until the train comes to a complete stop," the recording says.

"Boy, that was fast," Doyle says.

"Twelve-minute trip is all it is," Mike replies as he flips on the overhead lights.

Jonah stands up and turns to Doyle stretching out his arm, "Doyle, it was very good to meet you and working with you. I'm looking forward to seeing you again right here when you heal from those nasty injuries."

Doyle shakes his hand, "Jonah, it's been interesting for sure. Yeah, I will be back and with many more questions. Maybe you'll let me meet your associate then."

"We'll see if he will allow it," Jonah replies then turns and walks out of the cabin.

Doyle feels the train stop as the recording plays again, "Thanks for traveling with us. Please watch your step exiting the train."

"Come on Doyle, we don't want to hold up night-shift from boarding the train," Mike tells him, handing him his bag.

Doyle grabs his bag, "Thanks. I'm right behind you."

The two guys walk down the hallway of the passenger car then step off the train. They walk through a set of turnstiles then up an escalator two levels. During the ride up Doyle notices a group of people waiting to get on the train. About half of them have military uniforms on while the other half are wearing dress suits. After they reach the top of the escalator Mike turns right into a hallway that has elevator doors every one-hundred feet or so.

"These elevators go directly into our homes, every home in the subdivision has one. This is a gated community, everyone that lives here works at the underground base. This entire area is monitored twen-

ty-four-seven," explains Mike as he stops at a set of elevator doors and places his thumb into a reader.

The elevator doors open and Mike steps in, "Place your thumb in the reader and then come on in."

Doyle scans his thumb then walks into the elevator. The doors close then a woman's voice comes over the speaker, "Welcome home Mike. Nice to meet you, Doyle."

"Thank you, Hope. That is her name Doyle. Say hi," Mike tells him.

"Thanks, Hope. Hi. Nice to meet you too," Doyle says to her.

The elevator takes only twenty-seconds to reach Mike's basement. After it stops the doors open and Hope says, "I turned the heat back up to seventy-degrees for you guys. Goodnight, Mike, and Doyle. Sleep tight."

"Thank you. Hope, will you give me a wakeup call at 0600?" Mike asks.

"0600 it is," replies Hope.

Doyle smiles, "Thanks Hope, goodnight."

"You can stay in the bedroom down here. Everything you need is in the bathroom over there," Mike tells him pointing at a door on the right.

"Thanks, Mike."

"Your ride is picking you up at 0730. I'll have breakfast ready at

0645," Mike tells him then heads up the stairs. "Oh, Leon is flying back east with you too."

"Okay, see you in the morning," replies Doyle.

He walks down a short hallway to the bedroom and flips the light switch on. He sees an empty room with just a bed, no pictures on the walls, and no other furniture. "I don't guess he's much of a decorator," he says to himself as he drops his bag on the floor.

0645 HOURS
PRESENT-DAY
MIKE'S HOME CALIFORNIA CITY

As Doyle reaches the top of the stairs, he can smell the bacon cooking. He follows the smell and the noise of pans clanging together to the large kitchen where he sees Mike cooking eggs.

"Good morning. I hope you like bacon and eggs because there's plenty," Mike tells him.

"Love them as a matter of fact," responds Doyle.

Mike dumps the eggs out of the skillet into a bowl then walks over and places the bowl on the table. He sits another plate full of bacon on the table then turns to Doyle, "There's decaf coffee over there, and on the cart, there is milk and juice. You can't have caffeine because they may want to do surgery on you earlier in the day than planned."

"Nice, thanks brother," Doyle says, grabbing him a coffee mug and pouring him a cup.

Doyle takes a seat at the table as Mike walks over and sits down, "Doyle, let me say grace really quick."

"Go ahead."

Mike bows his head, "...Amen."

"Amen...Silent prayer uh?" Doyle asks him.

"That's right. You have a problem with that?" Mike asks as he reaches out and grabs a spoon full of eggs and dumps them onto his plate.

Doyle shakes his head, "No, not at all."

"Now eat up, you don't have long before Leon will be here. Long trip ahead of you today but just do not overeat. Because like I mentioned about the surgery thing," Mike replies with a mouth full of eggs.

Doyle places some eggs and two pieces of bacon on his plate before the guys enjoy their breakfast without any talking. Just as Doyle takes his last bite, his phone vibrates.

"Looks like Leon is here," he says standing up and shaking Mike's hand. "Mike, I do appreciate everything you did for me out there, I won't soon forget it."

"Not a problem. I'm sure we will do it again soon enough," he replies, still sitting down at the table.

Doyle turns and walks over and grabs his bag then walks out the front door. He sees Leon sitting in a black SUV with the window

down.

"Good morning sunshine," Leon says, then starts laughing in that familiar high-pitched laugh.

"Good morning, Leon."

"We've got a plane to catch. There is a private airstrip just a mile away that we are flying out of. We also have a medical team onboard waiting for you," explains Leon.

"On the plane? I mean they're going to treat me while we fly?"

Leon smiles and looks at him, "That's correct. That's how we roll dog!"

"Dog? Since when did you become hip?" Doyle asks, shaking his head.

Leon lets out another loud laugh, "You're a funny man Doyle, damn I've missed working with you. Anyhow, they will have your leg and knee repaired before we touch down at Fort Bragg. Susan is already in route and both your sons will be there too."

Leon turns and looks at him, "You're one of our most important soldiers, only the best for you. Plus, we need you back up and going in a month."

Doyle looks out the window as Leon pulls out of the driveway, "What's going on in a month?"

"You my friend, are going to start looking into all these missing people in North America. We are working on a database that tracks

when a person goes missing. They are broken down into four categories."

"Number one is a crime. Number two is suicidal. Three is Trafficking, and number four is paranormal. One through three is not what you're working on, you only focus on number four," Leon tells him.

"What, like ghosts and shit?" Doyle asks, sounding agitated.

Leon again laughs out loud, "No, you weirdo. Paranormal also means beyond the scope of scientific understanding. Like what you have seen with these suits and at the underground base. That is why we brought you on this search for Corey Prine, to ease you into things that most people don't know exist."

"I wondered why I was brought in after we found him so fast, considering we didn't have to search at all," replies Doyle.

Leon turns onto a small dirt road and pulls out onto a runway, "There's our plane sitting down at the other end of the runway. This air strip is inside this gated community and guarded twenty-four-seven."

"There's no air traffic control tower or hangars, uh?" asks Doyle.

"We use the tower at Edwards. Technically this is part of Edwards Air Force base now," Leon explains as he pulls up beside the Boeing KC-767.

"I thought these planes were only used for refueling?" Doyle asks.

Leon puts the SUV in park and turns off the ignition, "They are, but this one was modified to be our flying hospital. However, it is still

listed as an aerial refueling aircraft."

The two guys step out of the vehicle as two Air Force Airmen meet them and assist with their luggage. One of the airmen helps Doyle up the steps and into the plane. The inside is very luxurious with large captain's chairs and two couches. A large monitor is mounted on the front wall with headsets hooked to each chair. There are two stewardesses that greet the guys as they board. Halfway back is a wall and a door with a red cross painted on it.

"Welcome aboard Doyle, I've been looking forward to meeting you, I'm Captain Trogden. We flew together once coming out of Afghanistan."

Doyle shakes his hand, "Nice to meet you, Captain. I'm told that a lot but I'm sorry I don't remember you," Doyle tells him as he shakes his hand.

"No worries, Doyle. If you would please follow Paige and she'll help you get settled in our operating room."

Paige, who was standing in the back by the door to the surgical room, walks to Doyle, "Nice to meet you. I'm one of the nurses that will be taking care of you today."

"I kind of figured that since you're wearing scrubs," Doyle replies then laughs softly.

She walks him to the door and then opens it. As Doyle walks in, he sees an operating table and three people standing nearby.

"Welcome, Doyle." the doctor says to him.

"Hi," responds Doyle.

"Now, I know you had a small breakfast this morning and that's okay. We have a new way of doing things. You will not be going under but will remain awake the entire time. However, you will not have any clue to what is going on around you, it will be just like you are under as far as you know. This technique is top secret so I really cannot say anymore. Paige will prep you for surgery and then we'll get started."

She motions for him to enter a small room to the rear, "Doyle, inside you'll find a gown to put on. Everything else must come off. When you're ready just press the button on the wall inside."

"Yes ma'am."

Doyle enters the room and leans his trekking pole in the corner then starts undressing. He puts the gown on then removes his underwear. "Damn, I hate being cut on," he says as he reaches up and presses the button. He sees a mist coming out of a vent on the ceiling before everything goes black.

1600 HOURS
PRESENT-DAY
FORT BRAGG NORTH CAROLINA

"Hi sweetie. I've missed you," Susan says to Doyle reaching out and grabbing his hand.

Doyle looks around and sees that he is lying in a bed with an IV in

his left arm, "Where am I?"

"We're in the Womack Army Medical Center at Fort Bragg," she tells him.

Doyle rubs his head, "I don't remember anything about the flight or the surgery. What time is it?" he asks her.

Susan looks at her watch, "It is four-fifteen pm eastern time."

"I lost over eight hours. Well, just five hours if you count the time change," he replies sitting up in the bed.

"Don't try and get up, the doctor said he'll be in here by four-thirty."

Doyle lays back down then reaches down and feels his leg, "It's not a very big brace they put on me."

"Don't mess with it honey," she says, pulling his hand away from his leg.

"Where are the boys?" he asks her.

"They will meet us tonight for dinner," she replies just as the doctor walks into the room.

"How are you feeling, Mr. Anderson?" the doctor asks.

"I'm feeling pretty good, just a little tired."

"That's to be expected, Doyle. You will be happy to know that your knee only had a few bone chips floating around inside. We cleaned that up and we also placed a small pin in your Tibia to help with the healing process. Fortunately, the break was a stable fracture, so it was

still aligned correctly."

"The knee will start feeling better in a few weeks, the leg however, will take six to eight weeks. Stay off it for the first two weeks then I want to see you again here at that point. If all looks well at that point, we will start you on a therapy schedule," the doctor explains.

Doyle reaches up and shakes the doctors' hand, "Thanks Doc."

"You dodged a huge bullet; it could have been a lot worse if you'd landed on it a few inches lower."

"I guess I got lucky, Doc."

"Well, from what I hear about you, you're almost bullet proof," the doctor tells him as he walks towards the door. "You guys are free to head home, a nurse will be in here soon with a wheelchair to help you. If you need anything just let my office know," the doctor tells them then disappears out the door.

Susan grabs a bag and sits it on the bed, "I brought you a change of clothes, babe."

"Thanks, honey," he replies just as the phone rings.

He looks over at Susan, shrugs his shoulders and then picks up the phone, "Maybe it's the nurse."

He places the phone to his ear when a loud high-pitched whistle makes him drop it, "Oh my goodness," he says rubbing his ear picking the phone back up.

"Hello," he says.

There is a small pause of silence before a voice whispers, "Hey buddy."

"Who is this?" Doyle asks.

"Come on Anderson, are you really this dumb?"

"Miller?"

"That's correct."

"How...did you..." Doyle starts to say before Miller cuts him off.

"Do you and Susan still call people you are searching for Manglers?"

"Yeah...why?" he asks Miller.

"As soon as I am finished dealing with the Senator, I'm coming for you Anderson! I am the Mangler now!"

Doyle looks at Susan as the phone call disconnects.

"That was Miller?" she asks.

"It was...I guess."

Doyle turns and looks out the window. The sun is starting to set as the sky turns a pale shade of orange with dark lines stretched across the winter canvas. "I'm going to have to start at Miller's last known position..."

CALI-
FORNIA
CITY

THE MANGLER SERIES
STEVEN GALE

THE MANGLER - BOOK 1

Doyle thought life would slow down since he and Susan retired to Fontana Lake, North Carolina. He would continue to work with search and rescue teams and forget about the war deployments to Iraq and Afghanistan. However, this ex-Army Ranger would soon find out that the Smoky Mountains and Afghanistan have more things in common than what appears — thrown into the search for a missing young boy, the horrors of war quickly come back into focus. Doyle, racing against time to find the missing boy finds something very few people know exists. The rules-of-engagement seem always to be working against him.

LAST KNOWN POSITION - BOOK 2

Now part of the Patriots group, Doyle hopes to get answers to many of the mysteries he's encountered in the forest during SARs. His first assignment will send him to California in search of a scientist who doesn't want to be found.

However, the search is not what it appears to be. He has walked into a trap set by his archnemesis, Miller. Injured and weak, Doyle is now in a fight for his life. The quest for answers has only brought about many more questions.

Returning to an Air Force base from his enlistment days, he is allowed to see into a world he never knew existed. His view of the world will never be the same...

VISIT STEVEN-GALE.COM
ALSO AVAILABALE ON AMAZON

www.ingramcontent.com/pod-product-compliance
Lightning Source LLC
LaVergne TN
LVHW010614100826
845148LV00014B/2961

* 9 7 8 1 7 3 6 7 4 8 7 0 1 *